Richard V. Baker

Becky
A Tale of Two Girls

Copyright © 2023 Richard V. Baker

All rights reserved. No part of this book may be reproduced or transmitted in any form or by any means, electronic or mechanical, including photocopying, recording or by any information storage and retrieval system without permission in writing from the publisher.

Bamboo Press—Boston, MA
ISBN: 979-8-218-27678-2
Library of Congress Control Number: 2023917460
Title: *Becky: A Tale of Two Girls*
Author: Richard V. Baker
Digital distribution | 2023
Paperback | 2023

This is a work of fiction. The characters, names, incidents, places, and dialogue are products of the author's imagination, and are not to be construed as real.

Dedication

To the Lord above for his grace and mercy, and for giving me the strength to finish this book through difficult times.

To my Nana and Grandmother for their matriarchal wisdom and faith, and my Mother and Father for their everlasting love, diligence, and support.

For my two daughters that inspire my writing and give me a different perspective of life.

To Dr. Martin Williams who saved more than just the physical parts of my life, but also inspired me to continue on this path.

Chapter I
The Color of Trash

There was a time in this country when color was important, even in the days of black and white television, and the importance of your color was evident every day with a segregated country. There were harsh laws in this country for people of color, including the Indians, and those laws were strictly enforced, or left to the discretion of the racist white people who made the laws. After World War II the country had become an industrialized nation, but the separation between black and white people was a staple for this country since the Civil War, and the Indians were treated like beggars on reservations. They would breathe the same air and walk the same ground that God gave us all, but white people wouldn't even swim in the same ocean as black people, let alone eat or live next to them. There were white people in the country that knew black people all their lives, but were taught to never trust or respect black people, including the Indians, and to never let a 'colored' man get too 'fond' of their white women.

The separation of color was very prevalent in midwestern Indiana during the 1950' and 60's, and the Klu Klux Klan was still a powerful presence that enforced the separation of the colored races and the prosperity of the white race, while there were still some whites that were just as poor as some black sharecroppers, but thought they were in a better class of people because they were white. There was a story told in Sometime, Indiana about a woman who came from the East Coast to live in the midwest with her husband and children, and how she had a hard time doing her laundry around town. When her friends asked her why she was having a hard time doing her laundry, she told them that she had to go to separate laundromats to wash her 'Whites only' clothes, then to a separate laundromat to wash her 'Colored only' clothes. She was a woman that was not familiar with segregation and did not want to learn it from her neighbors, when she finally decided to do her laundry by the creek on her land, with her husband and children and no segregation.

Hate, and the separation of the races is a man made institution that is taught and indoctrinated into people, and most of those people being children. The children were brought up in a society where they couldn't even go to school together, let alone be friends, but two girls in midwest Indiana didn't care about what society said they shouldn't be, they just wanted to be friends. They met while taking out the trash on a mid-November evening in 1963 after the assassination of President Kennedy when they were both ten years old, and would glance at each other from a thin wired fence as they went to empty their trash in separate dumpsters. When they talked to each other while taking out the trash at night they would look around at their surroundings as if they were doing something wrong, then briefly talk about their lives with only a thin wired fence separating them, as they walked up a slope to throw out the trash. The two of them would talk about the tragedy of the President being shot and killed, and how he seemed to be a nice young President that wanted blacks and whites to get along. When they had time the two girls would briefly talk about what schools they went to and how nice it would be if they could go to the same school, and sometimes talk about their parents and how 'crazy' they were.

Part I
Troubled people.

Most children come from troubled parents, and most of the people they are around are troubled too, and those troubles can come from society or from within. Becky LeeAnn Black Rollins was the daughter of James Rollins and Dahlia Black and was five-feet, nine-inches tall by the time she was ten years old, but already had an old soul with a calm reserve. Becky's parents were former All-State champions in both basketball and track and field and Becky inherited their natural abilities, as she was a gifted athlete in both sports at an early age. She was a slender black girl, but wiry and tough, with long curly black hair and green eyes that she got from her mother and was the best basketball player for Sonoma Middle School. After their glory days of sports were over, James and Dahlia became 'big time' drug dealers and owners of some properties in the black part of the 'anas' but were troubled people, as James Rollins drank too much and was paranoid of white people trying to kill him, and Dahlia hardly being around as she chased her dream of going to Egypt via Illinois. Becky always maintained a calm exterior and seemed to have situations under control, but would take her aggressions out on the basketball court and even hurt some of her own teammates in practice. If it wasn't hard enough being black in midwest Indiana, it was especially hard for Becky because of her height and was called the worst things a person could possibly be called, even if she was only ten years old. Becky didn't go without discipline at home, as James would give her mild spankings but stopped when she was about nine years old, while her mother gave her 'ass whuppins' with a leather belt, which made Becky resent her. When James and Dahlia weren't being parents, Becky was watched over by a woman called Ms. Sheila, who was the same age as Dahlia and her best friend but had fallen on hard times after a traumatic incident in the town of Sometime, ending her basketball dreams.

Rebeca Stanwyck Dean Van Meter was a likable girl but had very few friends, except for her babysitter Abigail 'Sue' Burd whom she considered a big sister and had been watching over her since she was a little girl. Rebeca was a spunky girl with long brown hair down to her backside and big brown sympathetic eyes, with freckles to match her temper and would have fights with girls and boys in Aurora Middle School for calling her 'crazy girl' or 'Becky'! She was called 'crazy girl' because of her mothers' erratic, impulsive behavior and frequent arrests throughout the 'anas,' and her father being a careless fornicator of young girls. When she wasn't being troubled by her fathers'' lack of control or her mothers' mental illness, Rebeca liked to play basketball in school and take her aggressions out on the basketball court.

Both of their parents were troubled people, and most of the grown people they knew throughout the 'anas' were troubled also, casually talking about lynching blacks and what to do with white people that caused trouble. It was a summer evening in 1964 during racial tensions in Indiana, when even some white people were having a hard time getting along with each other, that Becky and Rebeca found themselves talking to each other between the thin wired fence that separated their backyards while taking out the trash. They shared with each other that most of their problems in life were caused by society, or the troubled people they lived with.

Part II
A friend in the distance.

There were many times during their brief seasons as young girls living on opposite sides of each other, with their friendship only separated by a thin wired fence and the laws of society, that Becky and Rebeca were the 'women' of the house because of their troubled parents. On some days and nights when they were taking out the trash, they noticed a girl off in the distance throwing her trash away in a make-shift landfill, just a stone's throw away from where they were. Rebeca asked Becky if she knew the girl?

"I think her name is Sara, and she might be Indian."

"An Indian girl, Becky! Well, Sara is a nice name and maybe we should ask her to be friends with us?"

"Friends, with us? When did we become friends, Rebeca?"

"Well, I thought that it would be nice, since me and you seem to be the two people that take out the trash around here! Besides, that Indian girl yonder looks like she could use our friendship and both of our parents p much suck anyway, why not be friends with her? Do you want to be fri with me, Becky?"

"That sounds fine, Rebeca."

"Hey, Becky, is that short for Rebeca?"

"No, just long for Becky! Does anyone ever call you Becky?"

"Heck no! Rebeca, and that is it, no Becky here! No disrespect to you."

"None taken, Rebeca!"

"Maybe tomorrow, we can go out and ask the Indian girl if she wants to be our friend?"

"Maybe, Rebeca! I heard that Indian people can be very mean, even girls."

"What is she going to do, scalp us! She seems nice and we're the only friends we have."

"We'll go and talk to her tomorrow, Rebeca, alright?"

"Sounds like a plan, Becky! See you tomorrow, friend!"

The next day a heavy rain fell on the cornfields of Indiana, flooding the fields and streets and temporarily washing away the segregation of society, when Becky and Rebeca met to do their usual chores of taking out the trash. In the heavy rain they looked at each other with trash in their hands, not understanding segregation and the thin wired fence that separated them, then walked to empty their trash and went looking for the Indian girl. They reached the end of the wired fence line that separated them from being friends, then looked at each other in the pouring rain with the peals of thunder from the clouds above their heads, and went to find the Indian girl regardless of the laws.

Becky and Rebeca both tore their rubber rain gear while climbing over the thin wired fence, and as they sloshed through the muddy field of the makeshift pit for the Indians trash, they saw a lone figure sitting under a tree, soaking wet. Becky was about as tall as some of the trees and just as dark, and when she went around the Indian girl to put a blanket on her, the Indian girl didn't even notice. Rebeca walked up the slope of mud caused by the rain to frantically get to her, and the minute she got to her, Rebeca started chatting away to the Indian girl by asking her questions of where she was from, and what her name was, and if she wanted to be friends with her and Becky?

As Rebeca got closer to her, the Indian girl became apprehensive and began reaching for her buck-knife in her wet pants pocket, when Becky slowly and calmly put her hand on the Indian girls' wrist from behind to prevent her from pulling out her knife. Rebeca didn't realize how close she came to being stabbed, or 'scalped,' by the Indian girl, and continued to ask her what her name was, when the Indian girl finally mumbled that her name was Sara Blackfoot. Rebeca looked at Becky with a big smile on her face in the rain, and told Becky she was right about the Indian girl's name, when Sara looked up over her shoulders and saw Becky standing behind her, still hardly realizing that she was there. Sara suddenly got up and told Becky and Rebeca to follow her along a path through the woods, and when they did, Sara brought them to a cave to get out of the rain. Becky and Rebeca were looking around the cave and before they could start asking her questions, Sara had begun a fire that revealed everyone's features. As they gathered around the fire to warm up, they noticed that Sara had caramel colored skin and beautiful cheekbones with jet black hair, along with piercing hazel eyes and beautifully calloused hands.

Thus began a friendship between Becky, Rebeca and Sara Blackfoot, meeting together under a large tree and following the path that led to the cave, all the while looking around for prying eyes as they didn't want anyone to find their secluded place. a cliff called Aianta. They would discuss about as much as thirteen year old girls could discuss and had come to know each other for two years, sometimes feeling that they were the only three girls in the world. Sara was a half Cheyenne Indian and would teach Becky and Rebeca Indian words such as love, and friend, and told them that the cliff they were on was called Aianta, which means 'Moon' in Cheyenne. They shared everything with each other, from their troubled, distant parents, Rebeca's worries about her mother's mental instability, and Sara telling them how she had stabbed her uncle and nearly killed him when she was seven years old because he used to 'touch' her and no one would listen, that's why her and her aunt had to move from Northern Canada to midwest Indiana. Then came a sad day on the Aianta cliff, as the wind blew leaves around them and flickered the little campfire, as Rebeca told Becky and Sara that her mother, Dorothy, had been sent away to a hospital and may not come back home, and that her father Tyrus had to watch her from then on.

Part III
Too much love.

With the institutionalization of her mother, Tyrus Van Meter was ordered by the court to start being a more responsible father, which meant he had to stop 'tomcatting' around the 'anas' and disappearing from home for days at a time, which Tyrus resented and felt his freedom being shackled. Tyrus took his resentments out on Rebeca by treating her more like a tired, worn out housewife than a daughter, and besides keeping up her grades in school and having meals prepared when he got home, Tyrus also expected her to comfort him when he needed it. This behavior continued for a couple of seasons until one day as dusk was setting on the landscape, Tyrus spied on Rebeca one night while she was taking out the trash and saw her talking to a tall black girl, then walking across the field pass the segregated wired fence line and meeting an Indian girl under a tree, then the three of them disappearing into the woods. When Rebeca arrived home a couple of hours later, Tyrus was waiting for her and angrily slapped Rebeca, telling her that she was no longer to see the 'tall nigger girl' or the 'murdering Indian girl' ever again! When Rebeca refused, Tyrus told her that if she continued to see the two girls he would have her sent away, just like her mother was! There were about two weeks that went by and Becky would wait for Rebeca to take out the trash, but only saw an angry Tyrus Van Meter walking to the 'Whites Only' trash dumpster and give her angry looks, telling her to mind her own 'nigger' business and go in the house and do some homework! One evening on the rare occasion that both of her parents were at home, Becky looked out the kitchen window and saw Rebeca taking out the trash with her head down, and immediately grabbed some trash from the kitchen and went outside without saying a word to James or Dahlia. When Becky got to the fence she asked Rebeca how she was doing and the usually chatty Rebeca said nothing, not even looking at Becky, until Becky grabbed her from the other side of the fence and saw Rebeca with a swollen eye, like she had been slapped several times by a grown-up. When Becky asked her what happened to her face, Rebeca told her it happened in basketball practice with a girl, when Becky told her she was 'full of shit' and took her to a waiting Sara under the tree. They got to Aianta cliff and Sara made another campfire, waiting for Rebeca to tell them what happened to her?

"Rebeca, what happened to you?"

"I really don't want to talk about it, Sara! Too much love, I guess?"

"Too much love! Who needs that kind of love, with your face looking like a punching bag!"

"Rebeca, you wanted to be my friend, well now you got one! Did your father do this to you?"

"Yes, Becky! Tyrus did this to me, and other things!"

"Other things, that motherfucker!"

"Don't get mad Becky, I don't want you mad at me!!"

"I'm not mad at you, Rebeca, but something has to be done about this! People go to hell or get killed for doing shit like that!"

"I don't know what to do, Becky?"

"Atsidihi, Rebeca, Atsidihi!"

"What does that mean, Sara?"

"It's a Cheyenne word for death, meaning you should kill him!"

"Are you bat-shit crazy, Sara, telling me to kill my father!"

"Let me tell you something, Rebeca, if you don't kill him, he'll kill you eventually, like he slowly did to your mother! Your mother would have probably killed him if they didn't send her away, she was a strange woman!"

"Jesus in Christ, do you hear this Becky! What should I do?"

"Well, I'm not for killing people because God says not to, but I have to agree with Sara."

On the cliff named after a Cheyenne moon where they thought they were the only three girls in the world, Becky got up and gathered her smaller friends under her long arms, as if she was protecting them under her wings, and they hugged each other and had soft tears by the flickering of the campfire, not knowing it would be the last time they would see Rebeca for quite some time.

Part IV
Just another killing.

She returned home from the cliff of Aianta with the words and tears of Becky and Sara in her thoughts, but continued to absorb the transgresses of her father Tyrus, the same ones that he dealt with in California and Missouri. Without her mother's 'schizophrenic' protection and Abigail 'Sue' Burd off to school, Rebeca was left alone with the wickedness of a troubled man near the cornfields and to make it even harder on her, Tyrus forbade her to see the only two friends she ever had! When she did attend school it was mostly for basketball games and practices, showing no interest in other things outside of school, and it soon became obvious to those around her that Rebeca Stanwyck Dean Van Meter was a very sad and troubled girl..

A midsummer evening in 1965 had a hot, drunk and agitated Tyrus Van Meter seeking comfort from his daughter once more, with a resistant, but broken Rebeca relenting to her father. After washing off the vile act that was committed to her, Rebeca went down into the basement and sat in a chair by the furnace, then with tears glowing from the fire of the furnace, Rebeca wrote a letter to Becky with Sara's name in it. After writing the letter on a dusty table by the chair and addressing it to; **% Becky Black Rollins, Sometime, Ind.** Rebeca went behind an old dresser and got the hidden shotgun where her mother hid it, telling her when she was younger, "Just in case the Ku Klux Klan comes 'knockin' on my door one day!" She loaded the shotgun with two dusty shells and walked upstairs from the basement, leaving her tears and the letter for Becky on the dusty table by the furnace.

Rebeca went into her father's room and sat in a chair by the window, waiting for him to get out of the shower and knowing she'd probably never see Becky or Sara again, but kept thinking of the word Sara had said to her, 'Atsidihi,' to kill, or he will kill you, eventually! Tyrus came out of the shower and found his daughter looking at him with dispassionate brown eyes, and a shotgun in her hands, and told Rebeca that he loved her and her mother, Dorothy, and told her to put the shotgun away as he was getting dressed! Rebeca got up from the chair and walked over to Tyrus as if to hug him and apologize, and as Tyrus held his arms out to 'comfort' her, Rebeca pointed the shotgun at him and shot him in the chest! Tyrus Van Meter fell to the floor from the shotgun blast and looked up at Rebeca in utter astonishment, gasping for air as he lay on the bedroom floor bleeding, then said to her, "You're just like your mother, you crazy little bitch! I loved your mother, once!" Rebeca put another shell in the shotgun, then said to her father, "You never loved my mother this much!," then shot Tyrus again and ended her nightmare by the separated thin wired fence. She sat on the bed he used to share with her mother and waited for him to die, and when he did, Rebeca called the police from the phone in the bedroom and told the 911 dispatcher that she had just killed her father.

With the flashing of red lights that descended upon her quaint little house, Rebeca sat outside on her porch as neighbors, both black and white, began to gather around to find out what happened? Sara Blackfoot saw the redlights from a distance and ran across the landfill and uneven field to see what she already knew, that Rebeca did what they talked about on the Aianta cliff and killed her father! When she got to the crowd, there were people that were more surprised to see an Indian girl out of her 'area,' than the little white girl that just shot her father. Sara eventually found Becky in the crowd and they stood next to each other, as the police handcuffed Rebeca and led her into the back of a police car. A long white car with a red cross on the side of its doors came and took Tyrus' dead body out of the house, as the neighbors stood around and gasped in horror and talked about how such a sweet, thirteen year old girl could kill her father?

The police car was pulling away and Rebeca was looking at Becky and Sara standing next to each other from the back window, and as their figures became smaller with the police car driving away, Rebeca sat quietly in the back seat and stared out the window. The police officer driving the car asked her why she shot and killed her father, when Rebeca looked at the police officer in the rearview mirror with her brown eyes welled up with tears, and told the officer, "Atsidihi, it's just another killing!"

Part V
A dire place to be.

Regardless of the reason or the motive, the court in the town of Sometime sentenced Rebeca to an indiscriminate amount of time and sent her to The Reformatory for Wayward Girls, in the desolate town of Dire. The town of Dire was a barren, desolate place where the sun rarely shined and if it did, it was hidden behind the clouds. Some folks in the 'anas' said that the people who lived in the town were in 'dire' need, and that if you got sent there for any reason, it was pretty much the end of the line for a person. The Reformatory was a large, gray concrete building that seemed invisible with the grayness of the clouds, and it housed about two hundred young girls that ranged in age from ten to eighteen years old. Once Rebeca got settled at the Reformatory, she was surprised to see that the Reformatory was integrated as she watched black, white, Indian, and some Chinese girls walking around and talking with each other, without anyone telling them not to talk to each other because of their race. Rebeca looked around to see if she could find a tall black girl and an Indian girl that wouldn't 'scalp' her, and maybe become friends with them. Without finding anyone to replace Becky and Sara, Rebeca would retreat to her cell or the library and write letters to her friends that she already missed.

Chapter II
Post Scriptum

The summer settled into fall and the leaves began to blow around again, with Becky and Sara still meeting each other on Aianta cliff, but not knowing where Rebeca was? Becky would tell Sara how she wished they could go to school together, but society has special schools for everybody, like the white schools for the white people, the black schools for the black people, and the schools on reservations for the Indian people. Sara told Becky that people were wicked by nature, and that was why she stabbed her uncle when she was seven years old, and why Rebeca killed her father, but how they could take out the trash for them, and that trash has no color! In the Autumn of 1965 as the excitement of basketball season began, Becky Black Rollins was the best middle school girl's player in the country, black or white, and was preparing to go to Sonoma High School. Sara Blackfoot continued to live on the reservation type of housing for the Indian people and attended Benjamin Harrison Middle School, living in a modest two-bedroom house with her aunt, who was named Grateful because of her nature. Sara's mother was Humble Blackfoot, the middle sister of Peace and Grateful Blackfoot. She was killed by some men up in the Canadian Territory for trying to avenge her husband's death when Sara was five years old, leaving her in the care of her aunt Grateful Blackfoot.

After the killing of Tyrus Van Meter by her daughter for reasons that were soon coming out in the newspapers, fathers around the 'anas' and other parts of the country started treating their daughter's better. James Rollins was at home talking on the phone to a guy about going up to Chicago, when Becky came in the house and asked where Dahlia was? He told her that Dahlia went to visit her mother in Illinois because she was feeling poorly, and that she had a letter on the kitchen table and that Ms. Sheila might be watching her for a couple of days. Becky grabbed a piece of fruit from the bowl on the table and sifted through the mail, thinking about a big game coming up against a rival school, when she came across a letter addressed to her. In between bites of her apple and shifting her school books in her right arm, she read; *℅ **Becky Black Rollins, Sometime, Ind**.*, and immediately went to her room and asked her father not to disturb her for a while. She locked the door to her room as if something bad was about to happen, then sat on her bed by the window and opened the letter.

Dear Becky,
When you read this letter, I will be gone from Sometime! I remembered our talk on the Aianta cliff with Sara and she was right! Sometimes I think about killing myself because of what my father is doing to me, but I remembered what Sara said, "He will eventually kill you!" Tyrus probably drove my mother insane and had her put in a hospital, and said he would do the same to me!

I know where my mother kept the old shotgun and I think I might use it on my father, he treats me like I'm his wife!! Like you said, "People like that go to hell, or get killed!" Whatever happens after this, wherever the bad people send me, you and Sara will always be my best friends!

Your friend forever, Rebeca.

p.s. Don't forget to take out the trash while I am gone.

During the next few months as the year of 1965 was coming to an end, Becky shared the letter with Sara and they treated it like a Dead Sea Scroll, folding it gently and putting it into a box after reading it. The nation was talking about the assassination of Malcom X and what he stood for, with some thinking that he wanted all black people to hate white people, and others not caring. Soon after the Malcolm X killing was told by reporters on television and printed in the newspapers, Becky got another letter from Rebeca, but this time with an address on the letter.

℅ Becky Black Rollins, Sometime, Ind.
From; Rebeca Stanyck Dean Van Meter. Reformatory for Wayward Girls, Dire, Ind.

Dear Becky,
I hope you and Sara are well and still go to the cave and the cliff? I'm at the Reformatory for Wayward Girls in the town of Dire, which is no

town at all! The sun never shines around here and all the grown-ups look mean, but some of the girls are nice. I found the only desegregated place in the country, and it's in the town of Dire! There are girls here from all different races, most of them runaways or just abandoned by their folks, with no thin wired fence separating them except the ones outside. They are getting ready to turn off the lights for bed check, but you have my address and please write to me and Sara too!

Your friend always, Rebeca.

p.s. I had a fight with a girl for calling me Becky, no offense! It seems like I've been here forever!

Becky read the letter and called Sara on the phone to tell her about Rebeca's letter, and to meet her on the cliff the next day so she could read it. They met the next day after school and carefully read and handled the precious document, with Sara crying because Rebeca was in, as she called it, a 'Girls' jail,' and would probably never get out! After Sara read the letter she folded it with precious care, then put it in the box with the other letter and some of Rebeca's hair-pins. Now that they knew where she was, Becky and Sara vowed to write to Rebeca every chance they got.

To; Rebeca S. Dean Van Meter
Reformatory for Wayward Girls; Dire, Ind.
From; Becky Black Rollins, Sometime, Ind.

Dear Rebeca,

I hope you are doing well and me and Sara miss you! The people around town are still talking about what you did, and some town folks asked me and Sara if we knew anything about the killing? Sara told them it was 'Just another killing' or 'Atsidihi,' to a bad person! We told some grown people what Mr. Van Meter was doing to you and it got out in the newspapers around town, now some people want you out of the 'girl's prison'... Sara's words.

Sara and I still meet on the cliff and still feel like the only two girls in the world, even though a lot of people like me because I'm a good basketball player. It's like you said, Rebeca, most people are full of shit and the other half are just plain liars! Try not to get into any more fights and will write to you soon.

Your friend, Becky.
p.s. Did you know that p.s. is Latin for post scriptum?

To: Rebeca S. Dean Van Meter
'Girls Jail,' Dire, Ind.
From: Sara Blackfoot, Sometime, Ind.

Osiyo, Rebeca!

Osiyo means 'Hello' in Cheyenne, just thought you wanted to know. I miss you very much, Rebeca! Be strong and tough, like I taught you in the cave and on the Aianta cliff. You did a wise thing by killing Mr. Van Meter, he was a very bad man! We read your letter about the fight with the girl for calling you 'Becky' and me and Becky laughed about it, and she said you have some 'issues'? We don't go to the same school, 'duh,' but when me and Becky hang out, nobody bothers us.
It's our last year of middle school and I'm not looking forward to going to Benjamin Harrison High School. I heard the boys are pigs and have no manners! I'll take my buck knife with me to school every day and probably stab a rude, pig of a boy. Hey, they'd probably send me to the 'girls' prison' and we could hang out like we used to?

Write to you soon now that we know where you are,
Your friend, Sara Blackfoot.
  p.s. My aunt, named Graceful, killed a rabbit in the backyard and we fried it up for dinner. I gave a piece of it to Becky the next day and she liked it, until I told her it was a rabbit, not chicken! She threw up and turned green! Have you ever had bunny chicken?

Part I
Where the negroes' play.

In the 'anas,' regardless of the weather, kids would shoot baskets on whatever was made available where they lived. Indoor gymnasiums were a blessing to most kids, but other than that, they threw half inflated balls into tire irons, old whiskey barrels, anything round from the junkyard, and crates from the packing companies. All of these things had to be screwed, nailed or bolted into a sturdy pole and most of them were telephone poles on the sidewalks of streets. In the black section of town where the negroes' played, there was a basketball court that was a black tar covered patch of dirt with a cut out milk crate nailed to a telephone pole as the basket. The area was known as 'The Park' and most of the middle school, and some younger high school kids, gathered there after school to work on their latest basketball moves and show off in front of the girls.

There were hazards to playing basketball on the uneven court with a half inflated ball, as the crate was nailed into a decaying wooden telephone pole around crumbling cement. A lot of talking went on during the games, but quiet and concentration happened when someone went up for a lay-up so they wouldn't land awkwardly on the crumbled cement and break their ankle. One day after school, Becky was walking through 'the park' with four of her friends from Sonoma Middle School, and they stopped to watch the basketball game on the milk crate court. The only girl playing with the three boys was a feisty, five-foot, four-inch girl named Tonya Staley who recognized Becky and asked her if she wanted to play? Becky looked over at her four friends and one of them said, "Go on, Ms. All-State," when Becky put her books on the ground and pulled her hair back into a ponytail and walked onto the uneven black tar court. Another boy entered the game to make it a three on three and they began to play, with the game getting physical at times because of personal emotions or being the child of troubled parents, but Becky showed her basketball skills and was impressing some of the kids in 'the park,' when one boy took exception to her talents. Their young tensions rose with the setting dusk of the day, when Becky dribbled the basketball to the crate for a lay-up and the boy that took exception to her skills fouled her hard, knocking her to the black tar pavement and on some broken cement! Becky laid on the ground unconscious and her four friends from Sonoma Middle School rushed over to her, as Tonya went over and saw blood coming from Becky's head!

"Tommy, what the fuck is wrong with you, why'd you hit her so hard!"

"It was an accident, Tonya, is she dead?"

"No, but she's hurt badly and bleeding from her head! Somebody go get some fucking help instead of standing around looking at her!"

Before Tonya could say another word, Wendy Monroe, one of the four girls with Becky and a member of the Sonoma Middle School track team, was running faster than an Indiana breeze towards the main road to get help. Some of the kids began taking off their 'getting ready for winter' jackets, putting them under Becky's unconscious body, when Tommy yelled out to a boy, "Elroy, put your jacket under Becky's head!"

Elroy told him that he couldn't because his mother just bought him the jacket and it was brand new, and besides, it was his fault anyway Tommy told him to keep his 'pimp' jacket on and went over to Becky, when one of Becky's four friends, a shy, nervous girl named Megan told them that she sees headlights approaching the park!

Wendy Monroe had run down to the main road and waved down a man driving a truck, who pulled over to see what the matter was with the distressed young girl. Wendy went to his truck and frantically told the man that her friend got hurt playing in the park, and that she was bleeding and needed to go to the hospital. The middle-aged black man told Wendy to get into his truck and tell him where to go, and that girl's like her should be at home doing their homework at that time of evening. Wendy told the man the directions to the park and thanked him for picking her up, when he asked her for her name and told her to call him Mr. Big John.

The headlights that Megan saw grew brighter as they approached the park, with some kids getting nervous because of the oncoming darkness of the evening and wanting to get home, when Mr. Big John pulled up in his truck where some of the kids were kneeling by Becky and looking like little deer in the headlights. Mr. Big John put his truck in park and took a sip of his gin, then lit a cigarette and walked over to where Becky was laying as Wendy went over to her three friends, Megan, Jackie, and Naomi and told them how she waved the man down on the main road. He looked Becky over and saw the blood on her head and took another sip of gin, then told them as if he were an angry parent that they should all be home doing their homework, instead of out playing in the dark and nearly killing each other! Some of the kids looked at Mr. Big John and thought he was a 'creepy old man' and had heard some stories about him, with Megan clutching Naomi's hand because she was scared. He took a sip of gin and looked at Tommy and told him to get another boy to help put Becky in his truck, when Tommy grabbed Elroy to help him. Elroy had to finally take off his precious jacket and handed it to the meanest girl of the group, Jackie Butler, who was used to fighting boys. Tommy and Elroy went and picked Becky up off the black tar court, being careful of the crumbled concrete stones around them, and took her to the back seat of the truck, as Mr. Big John ordered them to do it!

Mr. Big John told Tommy and Elroy to be careful putting Becky in the backseat, and to make sure that they didn't get any blood in his truck because he didn't want to be responsible for a dead girl, then having the police asking him questions for doing a good deed! Elroy finished putting Becky in the back of the truck, only to find Jackie wearing his precious jacket and telling Megan and Naomi how nice it felt on her, then running over and trying to pull his jacket off of her. He accidentally grabbed Jackie's more mature pre-teen breasts' trying to get his jacket off of her, when she punched him hard in his chest and caused him to wheeze from his asthma. Jackie took off the jacket and tossed it into the air, which caused Elroy to suddenly stop wheezing and get up to catch the precious jacket before it hit the ground.

Mr. Big John asked them who was riding with him to Mercy Hospital, because he didn't want to be responsible for her and having people in the hospital asking him questions! Tonya Staley told Tommy to ride with Mr. Big John to the hospital, since he was responsible for what happened, and he begrudgingly agreed to go to the hospital and make sure Becky was alright. Before pulling off to the hospital, Wendy Monroe ran up to Mr. Big John's truck and thanked him for picking her up on the road, when he told her that if there was anything else he could do for her, just ask people around town because he was easy to reach. She gave him a shy smile and said that she would look him up, then ran back to be with her friends and talk about the day's events, as Mr. Big John drove off with Tommy to Mercy Hospital.

Part II
Perfect Attendance.

He drove out of the area known as 'the park' and headed for the dimly lit main road, drinking gin from the bottle and glancing at Tommy, then the rearview mirror, with paranoid, nervous eyes. The hospital was less than a mile from the park and while slowing down for a railroad crossing, Mr. Big John told Tommy to see if ' the little black girl' was still alive, because if she wasn't, he would pull over on the side of a road and dump them both off! Tommy turned around to the backseat and checked on Becky, telling Mr. Big John that she was still breathing, but to drive faster and ignore the speed limit! They were getting closer to Mercy Hospital, when Mr. Big John turned the volume down on the radio and asked Tommy about the girl Wendy, and if she went to school around the county? Tommy looked at him skeptically as they came to another railroad crossing, then told him that she attends Sonoma Middle School like most of the girls, but she's always the first girl at the bus stop in the morning waiting for the school bus, because she's afraid of not getting perfect attendance.

Mr. Big John drove into the parking lot of Mercy Hospital and stopped the truck, then told Tommy to get out and find something to put Becky on, because he wasn't going to drive up to the brightly lit EMERGENCY entrance. The broad built Tommy pushed on the side door three times before it opened and got out, grabbing a broken-down wheelchair he spotted and pushed it to the backseat door to put Becky on. Mr. Big John did nothing, except turn up the volume on the radio and have another drink of his liquor and lit a cigarette, while cautiously looking around the hospital parking lot and telling Tommy to hurry up! Tommy put an unconscious Becky in the broken down wheelchair and pushed her into the EMERGENCY room entrance, where he met a nurse and signed a paper with her name on it and left. Tommy hurried to Mr. Big John's truck and got in then told him that a nurse took Becky to a room, when Mr. Big John sped off from the parking lot, faster than when he was driving Becky to the hospital, and asked Tommy very demandingly if anyone in the hospital asked him any questions?

Tommy told him that the nurse asked for the girl's name and he told her it was Becky, then left in a hurry before she could ask him any more questions, which seemed to please Mr. Big John and telling Tommy that the best thing to do in situations like that is to keep his mouth shut! It began to rain and Mr. Big John drove his ashtray of a truck down the same road he took going to the hospital, looking out for railroad crossings and flashing blue lights, when he asked Tommy exactly where the girl named Wendy waited for the school bus in the morning? He became nervous of the much older, stronger man and noticed the full ashtray with empty liquor bottles on the driver side floor, with some rope and a knife between the gas and brake of the car, then told him the same thing as to where they all waited for the school bus, at the bus stop by the park. The rain started to get heavier and obstruct his view from driving, when Mr. Big John pulled over to the side of a road and told Tommy to get out! Tommy looked at the rain coming down and told Mr. Big John that he could just drop him off at the park, when Mr. Big John asked him if he had any folks? The broad shouldered, scared young man told him that he had a 'Ma' and 'Pa,' with a younger brother and sister, called Cicely! Mr. Big John told him that if he ever wanted to see them again, he'd walk his 'black ass' in the rain and get to where he's going, and to forget about the evening's events! Tommy looked around in the rain, trying to decide which direction to take home and glad that he was out of Mr. Big John's truck. He drove off into the rainy night in his beat up truck, taking sips of gin and turning the volume up on his radio while looking at the broad shouldered boy getting smaller in his rearview mirror, then drove to the bus stop at the park, just so he could remember where it was.

A couple of weeks went by since Becky's accident in the park and while she mended at Mercy Hospital, most of her friends that were close to her were preparing to finish out their last year of middle school, and the dreadful awkwardness of high school. The news on television and the Farmers' Almanac predicted a terrible winter storm throughout the 'anas,' and in the winter of 1965, that storm came! The Friday morning storm in early December had knocked out the power in most places, and hurricane winds mixed with snow and rain made travel nearly impossible. Wendy Monroe woke up early as she usually did and looked out her bedroom window, noticing the nasty weather smashing against her window and the darkness of the house. She checked the television and radio for information regarding the weather, but more importantly, to hear if the weather would affect her from going to school. The power was out in the house she lived in with her mother and younger sister, but the grayness of the storm shone some light through her bedroom window, giving her enough to get her clothes together and be the first kid at the bus stop, as usual. She left the house without disturbing her mother and sister, and with her school books in hand she endured the nasty weather to finally make it to the bus stop, looking around for the other kids and thinking of maintaining her perfect attendance record. The wind began to blow the snow and rain in many different directions, as Wendy stood by the bus stop, alone, waiting for the school bus to come or at least some of the kids from school. She was about to give up hope about getting to school, and was more upset about not getting perfect attendance than she was about the weather. Through the snow blown wind, she saw headlights approaching and frantically waved her arms in front of the oncoming truck, dropping her school books in the snow.

The truck pulled over to where Wendy was waving frantically, as if he knew she'd be there, and rolled down the passenger side window..

"What in 'tarnation' are ya doin out here in this God forsaken weather, you can catch your death of cold!"

"I was waiting for the school bus and the other kids, but neither one has come yet!"

"Get in the truck before you catch your death of cold, I'll take you to school!"

"Thank you, Mr. Big John, I didn't know the weather was going to be like this?"

"Let me turn the heat up a little bit, so you can defrost from being out in the cold. Why are you going to school in this nasty weather, didn't you hear it on the radio that the schools were closed?"

"The power went out at my house, so we ain't got a radio to hear the news, and I'm only one class shy of having perfect attendance for the year."

"Having perfect attendance means that much to you, that you would come out into this God forsaken weather just to go to school?"

"Yes, Mr. Big John! I haven't missed a day of school in almost two years, and I run for the track team at Sonoma Middle School."

"How's that little black girl I took to the hospital, she didn't die, did she?"

"No, she didn't, she's still in the hospital because she got hurt pretty bad! Oh, by the way, Mr. Big John, thank you for picking me up that day, you probably saved Becky's life!"

"Has anyone asked you questions about that night, Wendy?"

"No sir, just Tommy telling us not to say anything about that night, and you driving to Mercy Hospital with Becky."

"You got any ' kin' around here?"

"Just me and my mother, and younger sister named Jasmine."

"Well, miss Wendy, it looks like you owe me a favor, seeing as I saved your friend's life and all!"

"What kind of favor would that be, Mr. Big John? I know it's snowing heavily, but this isn't the way to my school, where are we going?"

"Your school is closed today, so you're not going to school, and I'm tired of you 'fucking' kids meddling in my business, that's what you get for helping people out!"

"Please, Mr. Big John, just take me home, or at least back to the bus stop!"

"I don't think you'll be making perfect attendance today, miss Wendy!"

A few days later, after the storm that was predicted in The Farmer's Almanac had passed, missing person's flyers were distributed throughout the 'anas' for the whereabouts of Wendy Monroe and Mr. Big John.

Wendy Monroe/ Black female. Age: 13 years old. Size: 5' 4 inches. Weight: 115 pounds. Black hair and eyes, scar over upper lip. Family: Mother, Gertrude Monroe and sister Jasmine. Father: Deceased.
John 'Mr. Big John' Ewing/Black male. Age: 56 years old. Size: 6' 9 inches. Weight: 325 pounds. Black and gray hair with hazel eyes. Served 15 years in Dire State Prison for murder and sexual assault.

Becky had been recuperating at Mercy Hospital for about two weeks after her accident, with infrequent visits from her mother Dahlia and her father James showing up drunk, and threatening to kill the person that was responsible for putting his little girl in the hospital! Becky was laying in the hospital bed, watching the clouds slowly move by her window on a cloudy day, when a nurse came into her room and handed her a letter.

To; Becky Black Rollins, Rm#190.
Mercy Hospital, Sometime, Ind.
From; Megan, Jackie and Naomi
Sonoma Middle School, Sometime, Ind.

Dear Becky,
　We all hope you are doing well and getting better. Everyone is getting ready for high school, but first we have to get through Christmas vacation and a bunch of homework. It would suck if you had to be in the hospital on Christmas! Naomi and Elroy are boyfriend and girlfriend and he still has his fancy "pimp" jacket! It is not the same without you and we hardly go by the park anymore, besides, we don't play basketball on crates...ha, ha!
　Get well soon and stay strong, your friends, Megan, Jackie and Naomi.
　p.s. Wendy Monroe has been missing for a couple of days and a search party has been going on to find her. Megan gave the police Mr. Big John's license plate# AZ699 because she remembered it from the park. We all hope they find Wendy!

Becky read the letter from her three friends from Sonoma Middle School and began to cry, knowing that if Mr. Big John was involved; they'd probably never see Wendy again! She picked up a mirror from the table next to her and looked at her bruises, then cried some more because the doctor's had to shave a bald spot in her beautiful hair to put in stitches. With her best friend in a 'girl's jail' for killing her father and now the disappearance of Wendy Monroe, Becky began to wonder what was happening to the young girls of Sometime? While she was in the hospital recovering from her injuries, Becky got visits from teachers and coaches from Sonoma High School to check on her well-being, but also to see how their future all-state basketball player was healing. The doctor's told Becky that she might have to stay in the hospital over the Christmas holiday, which did not trouble her in the least bit, as she was enjoying the quiet and solitude of her hospital room, and with current events that were happening around town, she was in no rush to go out and be a girl in the town of Sometime.

Part III
Somewhere in Ezekiel.

Meanwhile, in the town of Dire, Rebeca got a lot of accolades and verbal abuse for being known as 'the girl who killed her father,' and tried not to fight with the other girls, remembering what Becky had told her but having fights with some girls anyway because of what Sara had said to her, and what she said being the reason she was in Dire. She went to counseling sessions with other girls who told their stories of running away from home, and living with alcoholic mothers and abusive fathers,' not to mention the uncles' that got to 'feely' with them. Some of the girls shared their reasons for setting fires to barns and killing livestock with axes, and having guns since they were kids and how they liked to go hunting for animals. During the mandatory counseling sessions at the reformatory, Rebeca never shared why she was there, as everyone knew what she did and felt no reason to repeat it! The facilities at Dire gave the girls opportunities to 'change' their lives around, but mostly to feel guilty about what they'd done and repent, by doing everything they were told to do, because if a girl got shipped out of Dire, there was nowhere else for her to go! Rebeca went to the school classes they had and played on the basketball team, which played other girls from reformatories throughout the 'anas,' and Rebeca was one of the best players in many games.

The closest she came to having friends that resembled Becky and Sara was a black girl named Precious Johnson, who was six feet and two inches and weighing about two-hundred and ten pounds and all of the backwoods of Missouri. There was a girl that Precious was close with named Shaquon Rutherford who was an Iroquois Indian girl that ran away from a reservation camp by the Canadian border, because everyone was drinking liquor and shooting each other and accidentally killing her seven year old brother named Quon. Before running away from the reservation known as Ezekiel Plains, Shaquon Rutherford plotted to avenge her brother's death by befriending one of Quons' friends. On a day when the dusk set in early on the plains, Shaquon was with other young kids in the woods hunting for rabbits and squirrels when she saw the boy responsible for her brother's death, she got close enough to him to shoot an arrow into him and as he fell, she shot a second and third arrow into him, killing him like a fallen deer. When they were outside getting some air from classes one day the long, black haired mysterious looking Shaquon told Precious and Rebeca what she told the police officers when they had her at the police station in Dire, answering their questions about why she killed the young man on Ezekiel Plains? She told the judge in court that she was avenging her brother Quon's killing and that it was somewhere in the book of Ezekiel that said, "Because you have not remembered the days of your youth but have enraged me with all these things, therefore, I in turn will bring your conduct down on your own head," says the Lord God, "so that you will not commit this lewdness on top of all your other repulsive acts!'" then after her soliloquy in court, the judge sentenced her to the town of Dire for murder. After a rainy day outside doing manual labor and watching Precious Johnson punch a girl to 'smithereens' for calling her a fat, black hillbilly bitch, Rebeca retreated into her room and wrote her mother a letter.

To: The Henrich Institute for Women.
c/o Dorothy Ann Dean Van Meter
Vesanus, Illinois.
From: Rebeca Stanwyck Dean Van Meter
Reformatory for Wayward Girls
Dire, Ind.

Dear Mother,
   I hope you are well and that the people there are treating you nicely. I also hope that they have you near the pretty Oak and Sassafras trees that you like so much, as I remember you telling Grandma Dean that's where you wanted to go. There was a very tragic accident, and the reason why I'm writing from Dire, the worst place on earth! I shot and killed Tyrus with the shotgun you showed me in case of bad things happening, well momma, bad things were happening and I had to kill him, or he would have killed me!
   I had two really close friends named Becky and Sara, you remember Becky, the tall black girl that we took to the beach and you didn't care what people thought, I miss that and wish Sara could have come. I hope to see you soon and keep brushing your hair like Barbara Stanwyck, ha ha! I will do my best to keep my chin up!

   Love, your daughter Rebeca.
p.s. I don't blame you for what happened and maybe, someday, you can explain all this to me?
I just found out from Becky that p.s. in letters means Post Scriptum, its Latin!

The Henrich Institute for Women in the town of Vesanus was a hospital that specialized in lobotomies, for those women with mental illnesses and a penchant for getting arrested for impulsive and reckless behavior. When the letter from Rebeca reached her in the hospital, the procedure had already been performed on Dorothy, rendering her like a meek kitten that constantly licked itself. A nurse read the letter from Rebeca to her, explaining how her daughter had killed Tyrus Van Meter with a shotgun and that she was 'put away' in the town of Dire. Dorothy briefly stopped brushing her hair in the mirror of her room, then looked at the nurse as if she didn't recognize her, then said, "That's a shame my daughter having to do that to Tyrus, I would have killed him myself!" then went back to brushing her long, brown hair and asking the nurse if she resembled the movie actress, Barbara Stanwyck?

Chapter III
Maybe it Was Barbara Stanwyck?

Dorothy Ann Dean Van Meter was the wife of Tyrus Van Meter, and the mother of Rebeca Stanwyck Dean Van Meter. Before she married Tyrus she was Dorothy Ann Dean, from an above average family with many ties and connections throughout the "anas," and stretches of influence up into Canadian territories. She was always a high-strung girl, which started getting her into trouble with the law at a young age. Dorothy was the oldest of two younger brothers and two younger sisters, which caused a lot of embarrassment to them and the reasons why they were very judgmental towards her. Besides her erratic behavior, she was bright and intelligent, scoring above average in her classes throughout her days in school. The one thing with Dorothy Ann Dean that put her above others was that she resembled the movie actress Barbara Stanwyck to a "t," at five feet, four-inches in height and slender built, with long brown hair and cunning brown eyes to match. These attributes got her out of some troubles, but it was also the cause of some troubles, as she slowly started believing what other people said, that she looked like the spitting image of Barbara Stanwyck, the famous movie star. After being diagnosed as schizophrenic in her mid-teens by doctors and psychologists, they prescribed her medications and weekly injections of morphine, which would be administered by a doctor. When she was seventeen years old she was almost put away in a convent for girls, by her father and the urgings of some town people, because she shot at three men in the back of her family's house with a rifle, almost killing one of them, with her claiming they were men from the Klu Klux Klan! It was because of her mother, the influential and hard-nosed Mrs. Mildred Dean, that Dorothy was not sent away to a convent but remained under her mother's strict, but flexible control. The Dean family had a large farm and other lands in the towns of Fairmont and Sometime, Indiana and were well-respected Pentecostal people. They were also known for having a famous cousin named James, or Jimmy as he was called, who became a famous movie star from the town of

Fairmont, Indiana. He was later buried in the town, not too far from the Dean's home, after being killed in a car accident. When her behavior stabilized, her mother would relax her restrictions and on a fall Indiana afternoon, Dorothy got into her green Ford sedan packed with some supplies and drove to Missouri, leaving a note for her mother that she wanted to see some of the midwest before it was gone.

Dorothy met Tyrus Van Meter in a bar in the town of Burnside, Missouri, after Tyrus punched a man for harassing her over a drink. She was taken by his stocky build and olive colored skin, which stuck out among the rather pale complexions of the local townspeople, and his crop of brown hair and serious brown eyes. They sat in a booth in the Sacred Crow bar, having drinks and telling each other a little bit about themselves, with Tyrus telling Dorothy that he was a minor league baseball player but got drafted into the Korean war, and saw some combat in China. He told her how he saw horrible things, fighting the North Koreans and how he got wounded saving his battalion. He told Dorothy that he was drifting around the country on a G.I. pension, picking up odd jobs here and there and ended up in Burnside, Missouri. While telling her bits and pieces of his life, Dorothy just stared at him with her cunning brown eyes while brushing her hair, not really hearing anything that he was saying, then interrupted him by asking, "Do you think I look like that movie actress, Barbara Stanwyck?." Tyrus was taken by the question, thinking that his tale of brutal combat in the coldest parts of Korea was much more serious than the movie actress, Barbara Stanwyck. When he told her that she bore a strong resemblance to the actress, this made Dorothy suddenly become interested in what he was now saying. She especially became interested in what he was saying when he told her that he saw Barbara Stanwyck on Sunset Boulevard, a few years ago when he was in California, in a coffee shop that he frequented during the day. Dorothy immediately sat up in the booth and stopped brushing her hair, and like an anxious schoolgirl started asking Tyrus questions about her, as if he knew her on a personal level. He told Dorothy that he even called his mother in Chino, California to tell her that he saw Barbara Stanwyck on Sunset Boulevard, but couldn't be sure it was her, when his mother told him that she met Ms. Stanwyck some years back in the early 1940's, and that maybe it was Barbara Stanwyck?

Tyrus and Dorothy left the Sacred Crow bar and walked towards her green Ford sedan, when she asked him how he got into town? He told her that he stole a car in the town of Wales, after being dropped off at a bus depot a few miles from the town and ditched the car a few blocks away. Dorothy tossed the keys to her car to him and told him to drive, telling him that since he was in the war in Korea, driving around Missouri should be easy. With the confidence of a man that fought in a war, Tyrus got into her car and started it up, telling Dorothy to get into the car so they could start their cross country journey across Missouri. Dorothy took her time getting into the car, so that she could look around at the scenery surrounding the Sacred Crow bar, with all the pretty tall Missouri trees in the background. They drove for a while down long, dusty Missouri roads and dusk was beginning to settle, when Dorothy went into her glove compartment and pulled out a fifth of liquor. Tyrus drove down roads in the town of Wales that weren't even on the map, looking for a place for him and Dorothy to settle for the night, while also sharing sips with her of the most dangerous white liquor known to man in certain parts of the midwest, Indiana corn liquor! Tyrus found a motel in a remote town, desperately wanting to get off the roads of Wales County, and knowing from history past the way of Confederate justice, and got a room at the Josey Inn. Once inside the southern confederate motif of the room, with an oil painting of Robert E. Lee hanging from the wall, Dorothy enlightened herself with the Indiana corn liquor and Tyrus' aggressive sexual advances. She began dancing in front of him in a provocative way and undressing, setting off emotions in both of them that would carry over past the dusty roads of Missouri.

    The milky clouded sun rose on the Josey Inn, with Dorothy and Tyrus waking up to a crime scene looking for a room. There were some broken bottles and clothes thrown about the room, with a broken night stand lamp that had a confederate flag on it, and the oil painting of Robert E. Lee slashed to pieces. After witnessing their wreckage, they both got themselves together to leave the Josey Inn before someone came and caused them trouble. They drove away like modest criminals, knowing that sooner or later somebody would be looking for them in Missouri for the fight in the Sacred Crow Bar, and the destruction of a motel room at the Josey Inn. Dorothy sat in the back seat of her car getting herself proper, while Tyrus drove down another dusty road and told Dorothy that he was hungry, suggesting that they pull over to a diner to find a place to eat. She could have cared less about finding a place to eat, as she was more concerned about how she looked in her compact mirror, while brushing her long brown hair and putting on red lipstick, telling Tyrus not to look back at her because she looked "a fright" and was getting herself ready. Tyrus pulled up to a diner called The Stolen Spoon and walked in with Dorothy, who had finally gotten herself proper, then sat at a booth by the window.

Dorothy looked around the restaurant, with her schizophrenia slowly creeping into her thoughts as she looked out the window, and thought of everyone in the restaurant as a bunch of lower class, ignorant rednecks, and she hated those kinds of people. A young blonde haired, blue eyed waitress came to their booth to take their orders, with Tyrus ordering three scrambled eggs, hash browns and a coffee and Dorothy ordering toast and a coffee. The waitress took their orders, then told Dorothy that she looked like a famous movie actress, in which Dorothy told her that a lot of people tell her that, then began brushing her hair. Tyrus was about to start asking Dorothy questions about what happened the night before, when the waitress came over with their orders, then blurted out, "Barbara Stanwyck, that's who you look like, that actress in Hollywood, Barbara Stanwyck!"

Dorothy stopped brushing her hair and suddenly rose from the booth, slapping the young waitress hard enough to cause her to fall to the floor, putting a temporary halt to the peoples' meals.

Tyrus looked calmly around the diner, keeping his eyes on a man to his right sitting on a stool at the counter, while Dorothy gave the waitress and the patrons a short diatribe as to why she slapped her. She was tempted to pull her gun from her purse, but didn't, then loudly told the waitress, "You're a greasy spoon, white trash, piece of shit! How the fuck would you even know anything about Barbara Stanwyck, living way out here in the middle of insanity, and trees, surrounded by all these ignorant people!"

Tyrus took a quick sip of coffee and jumped up from the booth, grabbing Dorothy by the arm and apologizing to the stunned patrons, as they made another hasty exit towards the car like criminals. He drove down another Missouri road, trying to piece together what had happened at the Stolen Spoon Diner, and in the room at the Josey Inn the night before. He drove for about an hour without saying anything, as Dorothy checked her appearance in the passenger side overhead mirror, telling Tyrus that the girl in the diner had a lot of nerve talking to her the way she did. Tyrus wanted to know more about the woman he was driving around Missouri with, so he pulled the car over to a secluded spot off the road.

"Dorothy, I saw you reach into your purse and get ready to pull out a gun on that waitress, after you slapped her! Were you going to shoot that girl, just because she said you look like Barbara Stanwyck?"

"I don't know, probably not! Anyway, everybody in that diner hated us the minute we stepped foot in that dump, I could tell just by looking in their eyes! Eventually, while we were eating, one of them probably would have shot one of us because that's what they do in Missouri, Tyrus!"

"You're from Indiana, how do you know that people in Missouri shoot other people, because of little differences?"

"Because that's what we do in Indiana, Tyrus."

"What happened to the Robert E. Lee picture in the room the other night, it was slashed to pieces?"

"I hated that picture, with his condescending eyes staring at me, besides, if it were up to him, we'd still have slavery in this country!"

"Ms. Dorothy, I don't mean to ruffle your delicate feelings, but are you emotionally unstable or just batshit crazy?"

"There are some people that would call me batshit crazy, but I'm not, just a little impulsive."

"Pulling out guns on waitresses in the middle of nowhere is not a little impulsive, Dorothy, and I was in the war fighting the North Koreans!"

"Well from now on, I promise to be on my best behavior, Mr. Van Meter!"

"Look, Dorothy, I'm no boy scout by any stretch of the imagination, but I don't want to be driving around Missouri feeling like Bonnie and Clyde! I have enough problems with Uncle Sam and the state of California, so do me a favor and no more impulsive behavior!"

"Listen, Van Meter, I already said I would be on my best behavior, like I was last night, remember?"

"I remember, Ms. Dean! You were an untamed hellcat ready to pounce, I'm just glad you pounced on me!"

"Yes, it was nice, Tyrus, not like my other times in Indiana. Since we didn't eat anything, let's find a place to get some supplies before we find another place to settle down for the night?"

"That sounds like a good idea, I'm hungry anyway and could use a break!"

With his questions about Dorothy's mental state still up in the air, Tyrus drove off to look for the next signs of life, hoping that when they found it, Dorothy wouldn't pull her batshit routine again. The green Ford sedan rumbled down another long stretch of road, while Tyrus' eyes darted back and forth for civilization and Dorothy Ann Dean, complaining under her breath about the rudeness of the waitress at the Stolen Spoon Diner. Tyrus spotted a large American flag blowing off the side of the road and pulled over, telling Dorothy to get some supplies when she got to the store. She began brushing her hair and applying more red lipstick, telling Tyrus she must look a "fright" after their long drive, then got herself proper and went into the store. Tyrus pulled over a couple of yards from the store, hoping to close his eyes for a moment while listening to Charlie Parker music on the radio, while Dorothy went into the General store to get supplies. She walked in as if she owned the place, but no one was in the store, except the overweight, cigar chomping cashier, which somewhat upset her, after spending all that time getting herself proper. The small store had everything they needed, so Dorothy got Bacardi rum, a bottle of wine and some chips, four sandwiches, some candy and a soda. Dorothy brought the supplies to the cashier, who rang up $15 dollars' worth of purchases, as Dorothy went into her purse to get the money.

    She stumbled around in her large leather purse, when the cashier said to her that she looked like the actress on the cover of Hollywood Star Magazine, Barbara Stanwyck, when Dorothy told him he looked like *"a fat, sloppy, redneck piece of shit!"* The cashier wasn't offended, and told Dorothy that if she wasn't busy later, he could show her a good time, because he never had sex with a woman that looked like a famous Hollywood actress before! While listening to the cashier, Dorothy thought about when she was younger and being raped by two men by Crimes Pass, in Indiana. She remembered that they raped her because she was impulsive and looked like Barbara Stanwyck, and then her schizophrenia began to take hold of her thoughts, again.

    Before leaving, Dorothy asked the cashier for a piece of paper and a pencil, which the cashier gave to her. She scribbled on the paper and asked the cashier to read it, which he did, thinking she may have left a phone number or address on it, then read, *Maybe it was Barbara Stanwyck?* The cashier looked at her, confusingly, asking her what it meant, when Dorothy pulled out her 32. caliber gun and shot the overweight, cigar chomping cashier twice in the chest, then leaned over the counter and shot him again!

    All was still quiet around the General store, as Dorothy stood by the cashier counter where the cashier lay dead, as if she wanted someone to come in and see what she had done. After a couple of seconds went by, she grabbed the Hollywood Star magazine and the bag of supplies and casually walked over to the car, as if nothing happened. The slamming of the car door woke Tyrus up from his brief siesta, as Dorothy told him they had all the supplies they needed, and to find a place for a night or two. Tyrus drove again, looking for another sign of civilization, when he asked Dorothy how much money she had? She told him she had $1,200 dollars and wanted to see the midwest, before it was gone. Tyrus told her he had $700.00 dollars remaining from his G.I. Uncle Sam payout. This combined, would lead to a series of emotional outbursts, sex and love in between roadside stops, drinking, crappy motel rooms and the food, the traveling, then the thoughts of Indiana!

The news travels a little slower in 1950's Missouri and other parts of the midwest, but when it does, it spreads quickly. The shooting death of the cashier was starting to get around, but Dorothy and Tyrus were on the outskirts of Missouri, headed towards Illinois. They stayed in the town of Joplin for a night and while inside an all-night diner, Dorothy began having one of her episodes at the table, when Tyrus slapped her, causing some of the men at the bar to put down their drinks. Dorothy thanked Tyrus for calming her down, when a couple of men walked over to their table to check on Dorothy after being slapped, a personal offense to certain midwesterns! One of the men asked Dorothy if she was alright, giving Tyrus a mean glare, when the other man said, "Dam, will you look at that! She looks like the actress on the cover of that magazine!" Dorothy told him that she "*Got that a lot from people*," then rose up from the table, pulling her gun out and telling the men to step away! Tyrus finished his shot of whiskey and again, grabbed Dorothy by the arm, whisking her away through the large wooden door, with Dorothy yelling at them, calling them every bit of white trash that she could think of! They drove off in the green Ford sedan, with Tyrus knowing that they would have to ditch the car sooner than sooner, and headed towards Illinois. The next morning, with the Missouri fog sweeping from the mountains, clouding the roads and trees, Tyrus came upon a neon sign that read Peckham Used Cars, and pulled into the dusty lot. Before the dust from the road settled into the lot, a man named Earl Peckham came out to greet them from his trailer, extending a hearty handshake before the car was even parked. When Earl Peckham saw the couple pull up into his lot in the rundown, dusty, green Ford sedan, all

5 feet, 4 inches of him became anxious to sell them anything. When he noticed a woman in the car, he even thought about selling the loyal stray cat on the lot, even though it kept the rats away from the trailer, because of the tough times in Missouri.

"How do, Mister! My name is Earl Peckman and I'm the owner of this here establishment! How can I help you folks?"

"I'm looking for a car! What can you give me for this Ford?"

"Well, it's kinda beat-up but we can work something out! Sorry, I didn't catch your name, friend?"

"Van Meter, that's my name! How much for the black 1947 Chevrolet?"

"With the Ford thrown in, it will cost you about $700.00 dollars, Van Meter!"

"Sounds good, Mr. Peckham! Is cash alright?"

"The only "right" I know, besides the Lord Jesus himself! Where are you folks headed?"

"We're going to Illinois, to get married! Isn't that right, Van Meter?"

"Ahh, yes, yes we are! We're driving to Illinois and getting hitched, Mr. Peckham!"

"Well, congratulations to the both of you, I'm sure everything will work out just fine! Would you be interested in a very protective cat for the lady, to keep her company on long drives? Women like such things, Van Meter!"

"Not interested in a temperamental cat, Mr. Peckham, I have my hands full with the cat sitting in the car!"

"That's too bad, she's a good cat! Well then, Van Meter, will you follow me to my trailer so I can give you the proper paperwork?"

"No problem! Dorothy, I'll be back in a minute, try not to get into any trouble!"

"I'll be on my best behavior, Mr. Van Meter, getting myself proper in this God forsaken place. I can't wait until we get to Illinois, so we get married!"

Tyrus came out of the trailer with the paperwork and keys to the black 1947 Chevrolet, with a smiling Earl Peckham walking behind him and a fortunate cat not sold, eating lunch under the trailer. Tyrus was talking to Mr. Peckham about directions towards Illinois, when Dorothy got the keys from him and began transferring everything from the green Ford to the black Chevrolet. Within minutes, she was brushing her hair in the black Chevrolet and ready to go, while Tyrus was still getting directions out of Missouri. They drove to the nearest gas station and filled up the car, then began the three-hundred mile drive to Illinois, with both of them unsure about what would happen once they got there. The black Chevrolet was driving good down another long Missouri road, when Dorothy told Tyrus that she thought it "odd" that the man at the used car lot didn't recognize her appearance, with Tyrus asking her if she was serious about getting married?

"Dorothy, were you serious back there at the car lot, about getting married in Illinois?"

"Dam right! You'd be proud to have me as a wife, I'll keep you outta trouble!"

"By the way, what's with the gun?"

"Shit, I'm from Indiana! Everybody got a gun in Indiana! You were in a war, Tyrus, where's your gun? This gun is for protection, against low-down murdering trash that would kill us like they were doing morning chores!"

"Well, you're right about that! Just don't go around pulling it out of your purse whenever someone doesn't compliment you, or there's a diner full of white trash people!"

"Well, Tyrus Van Meter?"

"Well, what, Dorothy?"

"Are we getting married, when we get to Illinois?"

"Well, after all we've been through so far, and you are a beautiful woman, a little impulsive and unpredictable, but I like you a lot, so when we find a town in Illinois, we'll get married!"

"That has a nice ring to it, Dorothy Ann Dean Van Meter, sounds respectable! I heard Illinois has very beautiful trees this time of year, Tyrus."

Part I
The town of Vesanus

With several miles behind them, Tyrus and Dorothy crossed into Illinois and looked for a town to settle into, as they would be getting married soon. Tyrus was driving and looking at the gauges on the dashboard, when Dorothy spotted a sign that read, The Town of Vesanus, and told Tyrus to pull into the town so they could find a motel, so that she could get herself proper. They pulled into the Crazy Moon Motel, and with a new car and soon to be married, Tyrus and Dorothy settled into room

#113 and began celebrating getting out of Missouri, alive! The town was named because of a religious backwater zealot named Caleb Solomon, who went about the town preaching fire and brimstone from his bible, telling all the townspeople that they were wicked and going to hell. He was well educated in theology and the bible and even spoke Latin to the "worthless Philistines" throughout the town, telling them they suffered from "insanus" and that they were all insane! There were many occasions when Caleb Solomon performed baptisms in the long running Redemption River, drowning some that he deemed to be unworthy of redemption. He wrote to newspaper people and religious organizations to have the town named Vesanus, which is Latin for insane or crazy, because of the town's wickedness. After pressure from a handful of groups, the townspeople agreed to the name, calling the town Vesanus and opening up a hospital for people with mental illness. The name of the town changed, but not the people, and by the year 1910, the people of the town of Vesanus had enough of Caleb Solomon. He was put in the Vesanus Mental Hospital for drowning 4 people and setting two houses on fire, killing 5 people and some livestock. In 1915 Caleb Solomon escaped from the hospital and went into the trees and plains of Vesanus, wearing an overcoat, hunting cap and overalls, and killed 7 people with farming tools on their properties, or in the town of Vesanus. The tall, lanky Caleb Solomon was eventually caught and put to death by electrocution in 1917 in the Vesanus Mental Hospital, granted by the very same people that approved the name of the town.

 Dorothy woke up early to a sunny day in room #113 and was excited about getting married, telling Tyrus she was going to find a store and a Justice of the Peace, so they could get married and have cigarettes to smoke afterwards. Tyrus told her to be careful and not to shoot anybody, then went back to sleep in the rustic, brown colored room, which had a strange picture of The Scream by Edvard Munch hanging in between their beds. Dorothy got herself proper, wearing a tight fitting yellow dress and black high heels, with her red lipstick and long brown hair done properly, making sure she had her gun in her purse, while thinking about the cashier in Missouri before she left the room. Once she left the room of the Crazy Moon Motel, Dorothy was not hard to notice by certain people in the town, with some women pulling their children closer to them, and some men with lust already on their minds. She spotted a general store and started walking towards it, when she saw a hardened mid-western man standing on a corner, and decided to go ask him some questions about the town.

"Excuse me, mister? I just got into town last night and don't know anything about this town, could you tell me where I might find a Justice of the Peace around here?"

"Well, miss, being the weekend and all, the county office is closed, but my cousin Oswald is a judge, he might do it for ya!"

"Anyone ever told you that you look like Gary Cooper, the actor?"

"Not lately, mam! You look like one of those Hollywood actress types. Have you ever been in any of those picture shows?"

"Not since Missouri! What about this cousin of yours that's a judge?"

"Cousin Oswald, he'll be at the bar tonight and if you got $100 dollars, he'll get you married, all legal!"

"What bar would that be, Mr. Gary Cooper?"

"The Insanus Bar, it's about two miles yonder from the main road."

"The Insanus Bar! It sounds like the name of this town, Vesanus, what does that mean anyway?"

"Both names are Latin for insane, because some crazy religious zealot told the whole world that everybody in this town was crazy, so they named towns, places, and streets after anything Latin for insane."

"Are there a lot of crazy people around here, especially in this town?"

"There's a mental hospital on the outskirts of town, called the Henrich Institute. That's where they send the crazy people from around these parts, but they have nice trees around there."

"What time should we be at the Insanus Bar, to meet Judge Oswald?"

"A good time would be about 9:30 tonight, after he's had a couple, and be sure to bring the $100 dollars!"

"We'll be there, Mr. Cooper!"

"You know, that really is my last name."

"Really?"

"Yes, mam! My name is Jebediah W. Cooper, and yours?"

"Dorothy Ann Dean Van Meter, from Indiana."

Dorothy finished her greeting and inquiry from Mr. Cooper then headed to the general store to pick-up more supplies, with the strange look of the townspeople gazing upon her every step. The minute she entered the store there was an overweight clerk sweeping the floor, and Dorothy began to remember the overweight cashier in Missouri and began feeling around in her pocketbook, for her gun. While her thoughts were flashing back to the incident in Missouri, two condescending looking women dressed in tight, uncomfortable looking black dresses came into the store and the clerk stopped sweeping, revealing a boy of about seventeen years of age. Once she saw the young man, Dorothy got her mind right and went about the store getting some supplies, remembering that she would be marrying Tyrus soon, and got a newspaper at the counter with her supplies. The bashful young clerk rang up her purchases and told her how beautiful she was, when Dorothy told him that he was a handsome young man, which made him blush even more and crinkle the faces of the other two women.

When Dorothy got back to the room at the Crazy Moon Motel, Tyrus was sitting on the bed smoking a cigarette and having a glass of scotch, watching the television and asking Dorothy where she was. She told him that she went to the store and everyone in town was staring at her, and that she had a very interesting conversation with a man named Jebediah Cooper, who told her where they could get married in the town of Vesanus. Dorothy was frantically telling Tyrus the details of her conversation with Jebediah Cooper, and how his cousin is a judge named Oswald and could get them married legally, but that it was in a crazy sounding bar, when Tyrus began reading the newspaper. He half listened to her ranting about a crazy sounding bar about two miles up the road, when he read on the third page of the newspaper, ***Police search for the killer of a store clerk in Achoa, Missouri! The killer may have fled to the town of Joplin. Please alert the authorities of any suspicious people in your local towns!***

After reading the police blog in the newspaper, Tyrus started asking Dorothy about when they passed through those towns, and if she accidentally shot someone in one of those towns, without telling him? Dorothy told him that the only person she remembered in any of those towns was the disgusting salesman that sold them the car, and how he was always leering at her when his back was turned. Tyrus was a little concerned about Dorothy's gun play when she felt threatened, but looked at her as a troubled, beautiful woman that looked like Barbara Stanwyck all of her life and had to protect herself... Besides, like she said, everyone in Indiana has a gun! The dusk was setting in on a mild day in the town of Vesanus and Dorothy was working on getting herself proper, excited about getting married to a complete stranger, while Tyrus grappled with telling Dorothy about getting arrested in California for having sex with under-aged girls in the late 1940's. Tyrus decided not to tell her anything about California, wanting a fresh start at 27 years old in the year 1952 and getting ready to marry a beautiful woman that most men would kill for, or get killed over.

When the evening came around 8:30, Tyrus had on a dark blue suit, shirt and tie, which he carried in his suitcase to look respectable on certain occasions, with Dorothy wearing a brown dress with brown heels and a long brown coat made from an Elk. They drove to find the Insanus Bar to get married, leaving the Crazy Moon Motel and the town of Vesanus in the rearview mirror of their car, then heading to start a new life in Indiana. When they entered the Insanus Bar there were about fifty people inside the stark place, decorated with Christmas lights all around the elongated building and wooden tables and chairs that had strange notches on them, with another picture of **The Scream** hung from behind the bar. The motley array of men and women from different towns all seemed to be getting along, and looked as if they could care less where you were from, just as long as you didn't get too close to them. Tyrus settled at a table with Dorothy and ordered a drink while Dorothy scanned the bar looking for a familiar face, making sure she had the $100 dollars and the gun in her purse when she spotted Jebediah Cooper and waved him over to the table. He walked over to their table and introduced himself to Tyrus, then told them to follow him to a back room for the ceremony where his cousin, Judge Oswald, would perform the marriage. Dorothy gave Jebediah Cooper the $100 dollars and he took them to a back room called the Skitz A Frania and met Judge Oswald, who was holding a drink in his left hand and a bible in the right. The portly, balding man wearing a black robe and glasses that hung on the brim of his nose introduced himself as Judge Oswald Cooper, noting that his cousin Jebediah would be serving as the witness to their marriage. He told them to join hands and began reading them their vows of commitment regarding marriage, as far as the State of Illinois was concerned, then asked Tyrus to place a ring on Dorothy's finger. Tyrus didn't have a ring to put on her finger and looked confusedly towards Judge Oswald, when Jebediah excused himself from the room and said he would be back directly, while Judge Oswald had them sign some marriage papers to make their marriage legal in Illinois. While they waited for Jebediah to return, Dorothy asked Judge Oswald how the room got its strange name and after a sip of whiskey, Judge Oswald told her that the room was named after a doctor that treated people in the bar that were not well in the head. The Judge told Dorothy, in between sips of whiskey, that the doctor's name was Skitzington "Skitz" Alfred Frania from England, and would occasionally treat people at the bar that didn't feel well, when he came to the bar at night for a drink after working at the Henrich Institute during the day. Dorothy was curious and asked Judge Oswald what became of the doctor, when he told her that the doctor was beaten to death by two women with small clubs, which were generally used to discipline livestock, because they weren't feeling well. Jebediah Cooper returned to the room and had a ring that he got from a woman in the bar, then handed it to Tyrus and told him to put it on Dorothy's finger, as to make the marriage official in the town of Vesanus. Tyrus put the ring on Dorothy's left middle finger and Judge Oswald pronounced them legally married in the state of Illinois, when Jebediah told Tyrus that he owed him twenty dollars for the ring, which Tyrus gave to him immediately.

Now a legally married woman, Dorothy didn't mind the group of people now streaming into the Skitz A Frania Room to wish her and Tyrus well on their marriage. There were some women, maybe three or four, that were asking Dorothy where she was from and why she was in the town of Vesanus? Dorothy told them that she was from Indiana and was traveling through the midwest with her husband, Tyrus, to see the sites and take pictures of the beautiful Sassafras, Oak, and Ash trees in Illinois. One of the women told Dorothy that all the pretty trees were by the hospital, not too far from the town of Vesanus and if she had time, she would show her how to get there. Tyrus was having another drink at his table, thinking about driving to Indiana and meeting Dorothy's family, now being the husband of their daughter that he met in Missouri. He never even met these people, and from what Dorothy told him about Indiana, they all carry guns! Dorothy was attracting the attention of certain men in the Insanus Bar, when a woman came up to her and asked if she had ever been in the town of Joplin, Missouri? Dorothy dismissed her, telling the woman that she had never been to a town named Joplin, and to be careful of who she goes about spreading rumors about her being in the town of Joplin. Tyrus had been in combat during the Korean War and knew that what he was seeing in the bar, with the aggressive behavior of the men and women slowly gravitating towards Dorothy, that it was time to leave the Insanus Bar and take his chances in the land of guns with people in Indiana. Tyrus finished his drink in a hurry and just like previous occasions, grabbed Dorothy by the arm and led her out of another establishment before one of her "moods" took hold of her, and got into their black Chevrolet headed to the Crazy Moon Motel to gather their belongings, with their next destination being Indiana.

Part II
Not my Indiana?

The newlyweds gathered their belongings at the Crazy Moon Motel, with Tyrus anxious to leave the town of people not well, and Dorothy asking if it was possible to stay for another night, for their honeymoon? Tyrus gave her a stern "Hell no!," and they left the town of Vesanus in the rearview mirror of the black Chevrolet, heading towards what might be Dorothy's Indiana. It was another hundreds of miles drive for Tyrus with his now wife, as he was trying to find out from her what kind of people he would be dealing with in Indiana. Dorothy was more concerned about telling Tyrus how she wanted to take pictures with her Polaroid camera of the Sassafras, Oak and Ash trees before leaving Illinois, and reassuring him that the people in Indiana are just like all the other God fearing people in the country. After driving for a while, Tyrus pulled over to a wooded area to stretch his legs and have a cigarette, while Dorothy got out of the car and stretched her legs amongst the Sassafras, Oak, and Ash trees around her, with an obstructed view of the Henrich Institute beyond the trees.

    Dorothy walked around the trees in circular motions, taking pictures of each one of them with her camera and some of the hospital in the background, then taking time out in between snaps of the camera to admire the fake glass ring on her finger that made her marriage official in the town of Vesanus. She suddenly became nauseous and began throwing up under a large Sassafras tree and while this was happening, she remembered from past experiences with girls in Indiana that when they got pregnant, they threw up under trees in the woods to hide the onset of being knocked-up with a child. There were memories that flashed through her thoughts of young girls almost getting drowned to death by their parents, or some overzealous townspeople in the Redemption River because the girl had strayed from God and became impregnated with sin, and had to be cleansed of the evil spirit inside them. The reality of the trees, slightly swaying from the breezes in the sky above, made Dorothy briefly think about the impulsive killing of the cashier in Missouri and if he had a family? She began to fret about what her parents, brothers and sisters, and some people in certain "anas" would think about her showing up after her excursion to the midwest, pregnant and married to a stranger? While fretting about tomorrows in Indiana, she remembered a passage from the Bible that she read when she was a child in The Gospel of Matthew, Chapter 6 verse 34, reading, "So do not worry about tomorrow, for tomorrow will worry itself, and each day has enough trouble of its own."

After reflecting amongst the trees that she loved, ever since seeing pictures of them in books when she was a child and had some peace of mind, Dorothy was ready to go to Indiana and confront what awaited her. Tyrus and Dorothy alternated driving the not so long roads to Indiana, occasionally stopping off at a motel but only staying for a night or two, without incident. While getting closer to the Indiana border, Dorothy told Tyrus that her family had land and decent money, but strange Pentecostal folks that didn't take kindly to strangers. She said that a lot of the people from the 'anas' still had Civil War ways, and wrongs could get a person shot, hung from a tree, or missing in cornfields. Tyrus told Dorothy that the ways of the country were changing away from the ways of the Civil War, and that you couldn't go around shooting and killing people, even lynching some, because of little differences.

"Mr. Van Meter, there are no little differences in Indiana. In Indiana, there are white people, Indians and blacks and the Ku Klux Klan! Differences are always settled one way or another, and God bless you for thinking differently about this country, but not my Indiana!"

"Mrs. Dorothy Ann Dean Van Meter, that has a nice ring to it! I hope we get a fresh start in your part of the country and your parents don't try to kill me the minute they see me, for marrying their daughter in Missouri?"

"When we get to Indiana, my mother will be glad to see me! I'm not too sure about the rest of my family?"

"Well, Mrs. Van Meter, your family is going to have to accept me in Indiana because I'm not going back to California! I'm your husband now, Goddammit!"

"That's right, Tyrus, you're my husband! This glass wedding ring on my finger from the town of Vesanus makes our marriage legal, I just pray that it will hold its weight in Sometime, Indiana?"

Tyrus was driving the black Chevrolet at a steady pace when he noticed that they were in the state of Indiana, then roused Dorothy from her nap to let her know that they were in her neck of the woods. When Dorothy looked around at the landscape where they were at, she felt something strange about being there, telling Tyrus that it didn't feel like the Indiana she left a short time ago. They pulled over on the side of a road so Dorothy could drive, as she knew the roads of Indiana better and was headed to the Dean Family farm, while Tyrus tried to get California out of his mind and adjust to meeting a bunch of strange people surrounded by acres of corn and Civil War attitudes. The day was setting into a cloudy afternoon when Dorothy drove upon the road sign that read **Sometime, Indiana 50 miles next right,** then slowed down the pace of the car and her emotions, not wanting her impulsive behavior or what had happened in Missouri to take hold of her when she finally reached Sometime, or other parts of the 'anas'.

Dorothy took a sharp left off the main road and continued driving into a separated place, a place away from the chaos of the outside world and finally reached the Dean Family Farm. Tyrus smelled the difference in the air and woke up from a brief nap, only to see something he only saw in Civil War movies at the theater when he was a kid in California. There was a large white house surrounded by acres of land, with livestock milling around in separate places on the property, being tended to by various people that seemed to know what they were doing, and the strange smell of moonshine in the air. Before they went into the house they got themselves as proper as they could, considering the many miles they drove, with Dorothy brushing her hair and telling Tyrus to let her do most of the talking. Tyrus asked her if all the land and property that he was seeing was her family's, when she told him, "And then some," when he felt that the tide of his life just turned for the better.

Dorothy walked up the small flight of stairs and knocked gently on the large Oak door, hoping certain people didn't answer, when her mother Mildred opened the door, with a shot-gun in her hand behind the door. Mrs. Mildred Dean gave her daughter a stern, but loving look and told her to come inside, when she saw Tyrus walking behind her, she drew her shot-gun and asked Dorothy who the stranger was? Dorothy waved her mother away and told her to put the shot-gun down and walked into the large house, full of confidence and telling a nervous Tyrus to join her in the living-room. Mrs. Dean put the shotgun away and went into the living room, where she and Dorothy shared a compassionate hug and Dorothy telling her mother who the stranger was.

"How are you doing, Momma? Where's Pa?"

"Your father's at the Club, talking to some of his so-called friends. Where have you been, and who's the stranger?"

"Momma, I got news to tell you! First of all I had a nice time in the midwest, but I couldn't stand the people, most of them were ignorant, white trash hillbillies! But I met a nice man that saved me from all of that, Momma, this is my husband, Tyrus Van Meter!"

"Dorothy, you're married?"

"Yes, Momma, and better yet, you're going to be a grandmother!"

"You mean to tell me that you went off for a couple of months to see the midwest, and you come back married, and pregnant! Dorothy, I'm just glad your father isn't here to witness this, he wouldn't handle it like I will."

"Momma, this is Tyrus Van Meter, he looked out a lot for me in Missouri and Illinois, from those bad, wicked people that live around those parts. Tyrus served in the Korean War and got lots of medals for bravery, he's a fine man, Momma!"

"Tyrus Van Meter, where are you from?"

"California, Mam. I met Dorothy in Missouri and we just hit it off, besides, there were men there that weren't treating her properly."

"You come into this house full of sin, and you want me to act as if nothing has happened! I'll deal with you like we always do, when times are right with the Lord!"

"That's not going to happen anymore, Momma, this is not my Indiana!"

Part III
A baptizing in the Redemption River.

Dorothy's parents, Jamison and Mildred Dean were devout Pentecostals and married at a young age, when the times of Indiana remained with a person for the rest of their lives. Upon marriage, Jamison and Mildred Dean were given some land by their parents, and with that land, Jamison Dean became a ruthless and well known man throughout the 'anas.' As devout a Pentecostal that Jamison Dean was, he was known to kill a man for an offense or have that person disappear into the vast Indiana cornfields. Mr. Dean was a wiry five-foot, seven-inch man with thick black hair and walked around with a scowl on his face most of the time, with a corn pipe clenched between his jaws. He liked to drink and gamble with his friends at the Elks Club but ran a large Feed & Grain supply warehouse and had moonshine operations in various places. Mildred Dean was a reserved woman with a light jovial side to her personality, which only her closest friends and her horse knew about. She was baptized in the Redemption River when she was a child and was almost drowned with the currents, which gave her a serene quality which people noticed about her ever since her baptizing. Most people throughout the 'anas' knew that the sometimes feisty five-foot, four-inch, brown haired woman solved disputes with a bible in one hand, and a shotgun in the other.

Dorothy had two younger brothers, John and Thomas, and two younger sisters, Helena and Aurora, who all treated her as a troubled outsider most of the time but were away from the home, either attending school or working at various places for the Dean Family Farm. Mildred Dean had shown great faith and compassion for her daughters' impulsive, reckless ways over the years, but now she was beginning to question those decisions, with Dorothy now home and pregnant, married to a stranger. The three of them sat in the living-room drinking coffee when Jamison Dean walked through the front door, slightly inebriated and humming a song, when he looked into the living-room with everyone staring at him. He removed the corn pipe from his mouth and greeted his wife, then said hello to Dorothy and asked her where she had been, and before Dorothy could get a word out as to where she had been, Jamison Dean asked her who the stranger was? Tyrus half nervously stood behind Dorothy, remembering what she had told him about Civil War attitudes in Indiana, when she introduced him as Mr. Tyrus Van Meter, her new husband! Dorothy proceeded to tell her father how they met in Missouri but got married in Illinois because of the trees she liked, and how awful the people were in every town they stayed in, then told her father that he would be a grandpa soon. Jamison Dean looked at his wife of almost forty-years with a bit of stern confusion, then hugged and congratulated his daughter with slight apprehension and asked Tyrus to step out into the air of the Indiana night.

Mr. Jamison Dean walked Tyrus over to a barn next to the house where he could talk to him in private, amongst the couple of horses present in the stables.

"What's your name, son?"

"My name is Tyrus Van Meter from California, sir! I met Dorothy down in Missouri and she seemed to be getting into trouble with people, so I was just being a gentleman and looking out for her."

"So, you married my daughter in Illinois, are you two in any kind of trouble with people, or the law?"

"No sir, we had a nice time traveling through Missouri and Illinois, it's real nice country, have you ever been there?"

"Not in a while, Mr. Van Meter! You know my daughter has mental problems, don't you? The way she's been carrying on the last few years, I wouldn't be surprised if she killed somebody in those parts where you came through."

"Your daughter can be an impulsive woman at times, but most of the trouble came from men because she resembles the actress Barbara Stanwyck so much, a lot of men would give anything to be with a woman like that!"

"Mr. Van Meter, from California, let me tell you something as her father, a lot of men have felt the same way about Dorothy throughout Sometime, Fairmont, and other 'anas,' but it's me and Mrs. Dean you have to worry about."

"Listen, Mr. Dean, I just want a fresh start with your daughter and I promise to do whatever it takes for that! I know Dorothy has some mental issues but we can work through them, besides, I just found out that I'm going to be a father."

"Mr. Van Meter, I don't have time to explain all the ways of Indiana, but I will tell you this, you're a stranger in a strange place and have married my daughter, which I give you credit for, but you'll do what I tell and ask you to do as long as you're in the 'anas.' If you don't, you can disappear like pig fertilizer in the fields, understand Mr. Van Meter!"

"Yes sir, Mr. Dean, when in Rome do as the Romans do! I did a stint in the Korean War so I know my way around things, besides Mr. Dean, if it wasn't for me your daughter would have been in big trouble in the town of Vesanus, Illinois."

"You seem like a fair man, Mr. Van Meter, that's why I'm going to give you a job at my wholesale plant and get you acquainted with some of the local people, with you now being my son-in-law and expecting a child. Remember this, Mr. Van Meter, I run moonshine from various places around the 'anas' and I expect your participation in these matters and if there's problems or killings, let me know. Another thing, Mr. Van Meter, me and Mrs. Dean expect you at church every Sunday, we're Pentecostal folks."

"What about Dorothy, won't she come to church with us?"

"We don't take Dorothy to church with us any more, it became a strain on Mrs. Dean and the other children."

After the private conversation in the barn, Tyrus and Jamison Dean went into the living-room of the house as if they were old friends, with Jamison assuring his wife and daughter that all was well with Tyrus and the Dean family. Dorothy got up from the chair she was sitting on and hugged Tyrus and gave him a kiss on the cheek, then asked her father what house on the property would they be staying in, when her mother told her that the house in Fairmont would be best, in case one of the other children came to the house from school. There were half felt hugs as the evening ended, with Dorothy and Tyrus staying in a guest house a short drive from the main house and once they got to the log styled dwelling, Dorothy immediately began asking him questions about what her father said to him in the barn. Tyrus told her that her father offered him a job at the family warehouse and wanted him to help him with some things after work, with some people Mr. Dean wanted him to meet. In the two bed paneled room with a picture of *Sunflowers* by Picasso, and a mounted Elk head in between the beds, Dorothy told Tyrus that he got her pregnant in Missouri and glad they got married in Vesanus and loved her fake glass wedding ring. Tyrus looked at his beautiful new wife and began kissing her and was about to have sex in between the Elk head with her, when Dorothy stopped and told him that she may have killed a man in Missouri. Tyrus told her, "We're not in Missouri," then consummated his marriage with Dorothy in Indiana.

There is a saying in the 'anas' that when the rooster crows, it's time to get up and face the day, or someone is lying about something. A cloudy Indiana morning had Mildred Dean riding her favorite horse, Gunsmoke, to the cabin where Dorothy and Tyrus were staying. They had a drink apiece the night before and were well-mannered, with both of them realizing that episodes that happened in the Crazy Moon Motel in Vesanus, Illinois wouldn't be tolerated in Sometime, Indiana, with Tyrus always thinking in the back of his mind about how you can become pig fertilizer in the fields. Dorothy met her mother and Gunsmoke outside the cabin and without getting off her horse, Mildred handed Dorothy the keys to the house in Fairmont, then asked Dorothy what happened to the green car she bought for her? Dorothy told her mother that the car was stolen by some redneck hooligans in Missouri, all because they said she looked like Barbara Stanwyck and refused to give the two men a ride. Tyrus came out properly dressed, which made a slight impression on Mildred, who then told him to meet Mr. Dean in a couple of days down at the warehouse to discuss working, once they got settled into their house. Tyrus graciously thanked Mrs. Dean for the opportunity to work for the family, promising her that he wouldn't let them down, while Mrs. Dean looked at him from atop her horse Gunsmoke with a skeptical stare.

With the family's orders in place, Mildred Dean was set to ride off, when she told Dorothy that she would be checking up on her soon and to not get into any trouble while she was with child, to which Dorothy reassured her mother that she would be on her best behavior. It took Dorothy and Tyrus a short amount of time to get settled into their four roomed, light green painted house that was sparsely decorated like a cheap motel room. Tyrus met with Mr. Dean in a small coffee shop just a few miles outside the town of Sometime, in a remote town called Klyde, where other people from the 'anas' gathered for breakfast and talked about their neighbors. Mr. Dean and Tyrus' conversation was but a breakfast and a coffee sip long before Tyrus agreed to do his bidding, starting as a laborer at the Dean Family Farm Wholesale Distributors warehouse. During the year of 1952, President Harry S. Truman gave speeches to the American public about the importance of defeating Communism and the Korean War, while Indiana held on to long standing beliefs in God and the Ku Klux Klan. One night while doing a moonshine run for Mr. Dean, Tyrus was taken into the woods and sworn in to be a member of the Ku Klux Klan, which he did with no resistance. A little time passed by and on a mild spring day while Dorothy was decorating the house in Fairmont, her mother stopped by for a visit to check on her and asked if she would like to go down to the Redemption River, which Dorothy hesitantly obliged to do.

They drove towards the Redemption River with Dorothy telling her mother the plans she had when the baby was born, while Mildred Dean listened to a fire and brimstone revivalist preacher on the radio in her beat-up black Ford truck. Once there, Mildred asked Dorothy to wade into the river to gather some floating driftwood and not long after she went into the river, her mother came splashing behind her and began grabbing her by the throat, trying to submerge her under the waters of the Redemption River. Mildred tried to keep Dorothy under the currents of the river, shouting, "God, cleanse the wickedness of my firstborn child, or may she drown by my hands in these waters!"

Dorothy rose up from the currents of the Redemption River with her mothers' hands still around her throat, then stared at her for about ten seconds while catching her breath, then saying, "Thank you momma, I feel cleansed again!" They waded onto the grass and sand off the bank of the Redemption River, with Mildred feeling pleased about her impromptu baptism of her troubled daughter, while Dorothy looked for a hairbrush in her pocketbook. Dorothy shook herself dry and began to brush her long brown hair, when she asked her mother if she looked like the actress Barbara Stanwyck? Mildred told her that she resembled her favorably, but that Barbara Stanwyck was a Hollywood scarlet and a jezebel to men.

Dorothy asked her mother to help brush the back of her hair and when Mildred finished brushing the back of her long brown hair, Dorothy turned to her mother and said 'Thank you,' then slapped her a distance from where the river meets the bank of the shore. Dorothy walked over to her fallen mother and slapped her again, this time even harder and dragged her into the currents of the Redemption River.

"You bitch, how dare you try to baptize and drown me in this river, knowing I'm with a child!"

"Dorothy, you've been wicked since you were born and that child inside of you must be cleansed of your wickedness! By my hands or the hands of God Almighty!"

"They tried that with you, mother, when you were pregnant with me, and again when I was a child! Dam you, don't you know what they did to me at Crimes Pass? I'm keeping this baby momma, regardless of your Civil War Pentecostal ways, this is not my Indiana!"

"Get your hands off of me, Dorothy! How dare you try to baptize your own mother, in my river! I pray that child doesn't come out as wicked as you are, and I hope that fake glass wedding ring and the man you married in Illinois hold up, like this river!"

"I've been cleansed and baptized, again, in the Redemption River. I think after this experience, my child will be fine when it's born. By the way momma, how does my hair look?"

Part IV
Seasons of rustling leaves.

Dorothy Ann Dean Van Meter and her husband Tyrus settled into a somewhat integrated part of Fairmont, with a small wired fence in the back of their yard that separated the white people in the neighborhood from the ***coloreds,*** who lived just yards away on the other side. With stories of combat in Korea and growing up in California, Tyrus was popular with the men he worked with at the Dean Family Farm warehouse, and being the boss's son-in-law didn't hurt his chances for promotion. The various men that Tyrus worked with treated him as the last person to get in on a joke, with none of them telling him the extent of his wife's' mental illness and the impulsive, reckless things she did in the past. Mr. Jamison Dean gave strict orders to certain people not to mention any of Dorothy's past activities, as he was about to be a grandfather and didn't want Tyrus getting into fights because of what people would say about Dorothy.

A spring afternoon in Sometime, Indiana was a time of harvesting and working on the large fields the Dean family owned, with Dorothy into her last semester of carrying a child but helping her mother with small things around the house, as they both had experiences in the Redemption River that seemed to bring them closer. They were outside of the house, looking over the large land that was their backyard and shucking some corn, when Dorothy noticed a bunch of leaves blowing from the cornfield and into the backyard, like a snowstorm. After the wind had settled, Dorothy asked her mother why leaves are always blowing around in Indiana, even in the summertime? Mildred Dean told her that leaves are always blowing around in Indiana, and that the Indians called it Seasons of rustling leaves and the rustling leaves would scare timid people and the animals in the forests, making for better hunting and killing. They had just come in from outside when Dorothy went into labor and before she could start brushing her hair or complaining, Mildren had her by the arm and was leading her out the door and into the black Ford truck, headed for Tempest Hospital a mile away.

The morning arrived with the birth of Rebecca Stanwyck Dean Van Meter, weighing a healthy eight pounds and some ounces, with a fuzzy crop of brown hair. With the birth of Rebeca there was some cause for celebration, with Mildren Dean telling people she wants to be referred to as Grandma Dean, and Tyrus being treated exceptionally nice by his co-workers. With the birth of a grandchild for Mr. and Mrs. Dean, Tyrus was sitting in the 'catbird seat' and was soon promoted to a foreman, giving him more access to the 'anas' and the temptations that go along with it. Dorothy's brothers and two sisters would stop by periodically to see their niece and ask her how she was doing, in a somewhat distant, judgmental type of way, which usually ended with Dorothy telling Helena and Aurora to mind their own business and to stop spying on her. Dorothy did part-time inventory work for her mother, who was becoming more attached to her granddaughter as the seasons of rustling leaves passed, while Dorothy struggled to maintain her sanity since the birth of her daughter three years prior. She was beginning to feel restless and restricted, as Tyrus was always on the road doing her fathers' bidding and no one in quite a while telling her how much she resembled Barbara Stanwyck, the jezebel actress in Hollywood.

They were a married couple but Tyrus Van Meter and his wife lived separate lives, as Grandma Dean watched over Rebeca in the big house in Sometime and Dorothy and Tyrus trying to maintain a marriage in Fairmont. Unlike the bonding they experienced during their travels throughout Missouri and Illinois, they were separately venturing into different parts of the 'anas' that would lead to serious consequences. A windy night and the rustling of leaves blowing behind Tyrus made him feel timid, as he was about to drive and meet a young girl in the town of Knowing. He started the new black Ford truck that he got for being the boss's son-in-law and father of Mr. Dean's first grandchild, and began to think about the troubles he had with young girls in California. He lit a cigarette and listened on the radio that Hollywood actor James Dean was coming to visit his boyhood home of Fairmont, Indiana, and he knew that the town would be buzzing with excitement and that he could probably push his luck, because he was married to James Dean's family. It began to rain when Tyrus drove off to the town of Knowing, fifty miles outside of town to meet a 'twenty-year' old girl named Cheryline Jenkins, to discuss getting her a job with one of the Dean family warehouses. With the rain coming down heavier than when he left Fairmont, Tyrus pulled over to the Blue Star Diner to meet Cheryline Jenkins, who was waiting outside for him under a stop sign. She got in the truck, soaking wet from the rain, and pulled her hat off of her head when it revealed a young brunette with blue eyes and grown features, but not looking quite 'twenty years' of age. Tyrus had met her during one of his moonshine runs for Mr. Dean and gave her $50 dollars, with a promise of a job and oral sex in the back of his truck. When she started shaking her hair to get the rain out of it, Tyrus told her it would be better if they got out of the rain and went to a motel, so they could discuss the job with the Dean family warehouse in peace, and that he had some food and liquor to make the evening more pleasant. Tyrus took Cheryline Jenkins to the Blue Star Motel and booked a room for the night, telling her it wasn't safe to drive anymore in the rain and when they got to room

190, Tyrus began offering her sips of Indiana corn whiskey to lighten the mood. With false promises of a job and corn liquored up, Cheryline Jenkins let Tyrus have his way with her all into the night, even in the sexual manner. A little after ten in the evening while Cheryline was taking a shower and Tyrus was having a nightcap, two police officers from the town of Knowing knocked on door 190 to ask Tyrus questions about the young woman in his room. Tyrus stood in the doorway of the room with an unbuttoned shirt on and half zipped trousers, telling the two police officers that the young woman in the room was his niece from Missouri, and he was going to drive her to see her relatives in the town of Lybel in the morning. The two older police officers stood in the doorway listening to Tyrus but when Cheryline Jenkins came out of the bathroom half-naked, they knew she was an underaged girl, with both of the officers having daughters of their own and looking for an underaged runaway girl in the town of Knowing. The two police officers arrested Tyrus for violating the Mann Act and took Cheryline Jenkins into custody as a fugitive runaway. They were both taken to the police station in the town of Knowing, where a police captain explained the Mann Act of 1910 to Tyrus and why he was being arrested, telling him it was originally called The White-Slave Traffic Act and forbid the transporting of a minor across state lines for the purpose of prostitution or other illegal sexual acts. The police captain also informed Tyrus that the Mann Act was passed in 1910 to catch that 'nigger' boxer Jack Johnson when he would bring white women into towns for sexual acts. Tyrus told the burly, pock marked faced police captain that he wasn't a 'nigger' boxer and was only taking his niece to the town of Lybel to be with her relatives, but the more he talked his California accent irritated the police captain and he put Tyrus in jail. The next morning saw more rain and Cheryline Jenkins denying to an aggressive policeman questioning her that she was raped, even though he found out through a missing persons' report that she was sixteen-years old. With no kin or relatives to claim her, Cheryline Jenkins was sent to the Girls Reformatory in Dire, Indiana and Tyrus got to make a dreadful phone call to Sometime, hoping that Dorothy would pick up the phone.

 Dorothy got the call from Tyrus and immediately called her father, telling him that Tyrus had gotten arrested in the town of Knowing over a misunderstanding, and had to drive there to get Tyrus out of jail as soon as possible. Mr. Dean drove his blue Chevy out to the town of Knowing in the morning to get his son-in-law out of jail, and with his first cousin Ezeckial Dean being the judge of the county, Jamison Dean knew he wouldn't have too much of a problem getting Tyrus out. After having brunch with his cousin and finding out the charges against Tyrus, Jamison Dean handed his cousin $5,000.00 dollars and within an hour in a 'kangaroo' court all charges against Tyrus were dropped and dismissed. Before leaving the town of Knowing, Jamison told his cousin Ezeckial Dean that a famous relative was paying a visit to Fairmont in a couple of weeks, and that he should stop over to Fairmont when it happens because a lot of movie cameras would be there. Tyrus and Jamison headed back to Sometime in two separate cars with two separate thoughts of mind about what happened in the town of Knowing, with Jamison Dean more concerned about a famous relative coming to Fairmont, and Tyrus thinking about cornfields and not wanting to end up as pig fertilizer. Before reaching the town of Sometime they pulled off to the side of a road and went into a secluded wooded area to relieve themselves, with both men thinking about what to say about the incident in the town of Knowing once they reached Sometime and Fairmont. Tyrus found a secluded spot and was making like a 'bear in the woods' under a tree with a newspaper in his hands, when he heard the click of a gun and looked up to see Mr. Jamison Dean pointing a double-barreled shotgun at him. With the rustling of leaves around him as he squatted vulnerable under a tree, Mr. Jamison Dean told Tyrus that he was not in California anymore and if he ever did again what happened in the town of Knowing, he would blow what little brains he had out of his head!

Part V
Where's Jimmy?

The incident in Knowing, Indiana was slowly fading away with Dorothy and most of the Dean family, as they were more preoccupied with getting things together with the people of Fairmont and other 'anas' for the arrival of James Dean, the movie star from Hollywood. Mr. Jamison Dean was a first cousin of Winton Dean, James Dean's father, and there were many times when 'Jimmy' stayed at the Dean family farm, especially when his mother died suddenly at a young age. On a brisk September evening in 1955, Dorothy was sharing some of her childhood memories about her cousin James Dean, telling Tyrus and Rebeca how he was always called 'Jimmy,' and was a rambunctious kid and how they used to be 'kissing cousins' in the back of the barn. Tyrus could care less about 'Jimmy' Dean or the big parade for him in Fairmont, besides, he never even saw him in a motion picture and thought more about Cheryline Jenkins locked up in Dire, Indiana than most other things going on around him.

On a Thursday evening in September as Dorothy watched over Rebeca, and Tyrus was doing Mr. Dean's biddings, she received a long distance call from California from cousin, 'Jimmy' Dean. She was excited to hear from him and immediately asked him if he's seen Barbara Stanwyck, which he told Dorothy he had on a couple of occasions and how much she looked like Barbara Stanywick and could be an actress in Hollywood. Dorothy was completely enraptured by her cousin's flattering comments, telling him that her husband was from California and maybe they could go out there to visit, then began brushing her long brown hair in the living-room mirror, as it had been a long time since someone told her of her resemblance to Barbara Stanwyck. He told Dorothy that he had a car race in California and after the race he was heading to Fairmont, when Dorothy told him that all the people from the 'anas' were throwing him a big welcoming home party. After the phone call with her cousin, Dorothy began to think about going out to Hollywood with her cousin when he left Fairmont and becoming an actress, while trying to forget about what Tyrus did to a young girl in the town of Knowing and what happened in Missouri.

The coming to the end of September is when people from the 'anas' get their rifles and guns ready for hunting season, and neighbors put aside long held grudges to store up for the winter. Throughout the towns of Sometime and Fairmont, neighbors and strangers would greet each other with distant hello's but always ask 'Where's Jimmy'? The towns were selling every magazine with James Dean's picture on them, even though most people throughout the 'anas' never even saw him in a movie picture show. The gossip around Fairmont, mostly spread by Dorothy, was that 'Jimmy' would be in town on the 28th of September, and some townspeople postponed their hunting trips because of the occasion. When the 29th day of September came around most people were constantly asking each other, 'Where's Jimmy,' then went about their normal day, but with anticipated excitement. What goes on in the world travels slowly into other parts, like molasses in the winter, but when it gets there it travels like a brush fire, and such was the news of the world when it finally trickled into the 'anas' on the 2nd of October. Now the many questions and false answers asked and given by people as to 'Where's Jimmy' were answered on television and the newspapers, ***James Dean, Hollywood Actor dies in car crash at 24 years old.*** After the tragic and sudden death of Fairmonts' favorite son, some people were heartbroken and mourned while others went on their delayed hunting trips and resumed their grudges with neighbors around the 'anas.' With her cousin's death from a car accident, Dorothy lost all hope of going to Hollywood and becoming an actress like Barbara Stanwyck, just like she had discussed with Jimmy, but now wanted to be a better actress, that of a good mother and wife, with a respectable reputation throughout the 'anas.' There were soon rumors around the 'anas' again as to, 'Where's Jimmy,' but this time when and where he was to be buried.

Part VI
The pretty trees of Illinois.

The gray, rigid ways of the country were becoming colorized with the dawn of the 1960's, and a young, vibrant man being elected President of the United States. With the colorization of America it highlighted a lot of things, but it was still cut and dry, black and white, and as clear as day when it came to 'color,' know your place! The segregation of races is a man made thing, and children don't know about 'manmade things' but only about being children. In the year of 1962, Tyrus was an unwilling member of the Ku Klux Klan and witnessed a couple of lynchings, even of some white people, and began to absorb the hatred around him, while Dorothy Ann Dean Van Meter could care less about your skin color. A summer afternoon was brewing with racial tensions throughout the 'anas' and parts of Illinois and farther, caused by the burgeoning movement of Civil Rights protests, when Rebeca took out the trash from the back of her house and saw a tall black girl doing the same. They emptied their trash in separate dumpsters and walked back to their houses, glancing at each other only briefly. While Dorothy played the respectable mother, Tyrus was having an affair with Cheryline Jenkins, who had been released from the Reformatory in Dire, Indiana and had a small apartment 75 miles from Fairmont. The Dean Family Wholesale distributors prospered during these times and with Mildred Dean dotting on Rebeca and Tyrus living his separate life, Dorothy's schizophrenia slowly began to creep into her thoughts of her solo trip to the midwest, and the pictures she took of the pretty trees of

Illinois.

With her days being spent as a 'single' housewife tending to her eight-year old daughter and Tyrus being gone most of the time, Dorothy put an ad in the local newspaper for a babysitter. A couple of days later a sixteen-year old girl showed up at Dorothy's house applying for the babysitter job, with gym clothes on and all sweaty after playing basketball for her girl's high school team. Dorothy invited her in and gave her a glass of water, looking her up and down to see if she was white trash that she didn't want to be associated with, even if she was a young girl.

"What's your name, sweaty little girl?"

"My name is Abigail SueAnn Burd, Mrs. Van Meter, but most people just call me Sue because it's easier."

"Why are you all sweaty, like you've been running around in a field or something?"

"I just came from basketball practice, Mam, and I didn't have a change of clothes."

"You play basketball? That's a boy's sport, you shouldn't be running around with boys playing sports, trust me."

"I play on a girls basketball team for Aurora High School, I'm a sophomore Mrs. Van Meter."

"They have girls basketball teams in schools, well no shit! Who would have heard of such a thing in my days, young girls only got dirty if they worked in the fields, you ever worked in the fields, Sue?"

"Not really, but I helped my mother out a couple of times in the backyard."

"What part of the 'anas' you from, basketball girl?"

"A town called Faulkner, just two miles from her. Mrs. Van Meter, can I have the babysitting job?"

"Yes you can, and I'll pay you $25.00 dollars a week. I need you here from the time you get off of school until about nine at night."

"Mrs. Van Meter, that's almost as much as my father makes in a month, that's too much money."

"Listen, sweaty little girl, most of the land you walk on belongs to God and my family, and from now on refer to me as Mrs. Dean."

"Yes, Mam! When do I start babysitting?"

"My daughter's name is Rebeca Stanwyck Dean Van Meter, but just call her Rebeca. Sue Burd, have you ever been to Illinois?"

"No, Mam."

"Well I have, and Illinois has the prettiest trees I have ever seen. I took some Polaroid pictures of them the last time I was there, I'll show them to you sometime."

"That would be fine Mrs. Dean, when would you like me to start babysitting?"

"Tomorrow, at about six in the evening! I have to go into town and meet some people, here's $40 dollars to get things going and don't show up here smelling like a barn animal, understood!"

"Yes, Mrs. Dean! I'll wash up at school and bring an extra set of clothes with me. Excuse me Mrs. Dean, but did you say that you were going to give me $40 dollars?"

"That's right, I'm giving you $40 dollars now and will pay you $25 dollars a week, is that a problem, Sue?"

"Sold American! Hot dam, Mrs. Dean, that's more than what most grown folks make!"

"You hush your mouth and tell people I pay you $10 dollars a week, you understand me! A young hillbilly girl like you walking around with that kind of money is bound to draw attention. You find a safe hiding spot to put away the extra money, and don't tell any of your sweaty little redneck friends either, they'll turn on you in a minute, you understand what I'm saying to you, Sue!"

"Yes, Mrs. Dean, you have my word and I never lie about things of such importance."

"You like the movies and watching movie stars from Hollywood, Abigail SueAnn Burd?"

"Sure do, Mrs. Dean, who doesn't like going to the movies!"

"Have you ever heard of Barbara Stanwyck? Do you think I resemble her in any way?"

"I never heard of Barbara Stanwyck, was she some kind of actress or something?"

With a high school babysitter making as much as some grown folks around the 'anas,' and Tyrus coming home only two or three times a week, Dorothy would go to remote towns outside of Fairmont and Sometime to have a drink and be impulsive, like she was in Missouri and the town of Vesanus. Within a couple of months, Dorothy was arrested on two different occasions for rude and lascivious behavior, and questioned by the sheriff of Faulkner County about pulling out a gun on a man in the Sundown Bar. Sheriff Brando of Faulkner County asked

Dorothy if she pulled a gun out on a man in the Sundown Bar, and if she took a shot at him? Dorothy told the sheriff, "Maybe it was Barbara Stanwyck that pulled a gun out on that man? And if I did pull out a gun it was for my protection, because those 'goat raping hillbillies' were becoming aggressive towards me!" Sheriff Brando pulled out a file report from his desk and looked it over, then asked Dorothy if she had been in the town of Joplin, Missouri a couple of years back, and if she had any knowledge of the killing of a store clerk? Dorothy told him that she and Tyrus passed through the town several years ago to buy a car, then got married in Illinois because she liked the trees there. Sheriff Brando told Dorothy that he thought she was a dangerous woman and probably shot and killed the store clerk in Missouri, and from reading her file he said he would recommend that she be put away for a while, but not for the murder in Missouri. The short, stout, very serious minded sheriff got on the phone, when Dorothy called him a 'white trash member of the KKK' and threw a small statue of a horse at him, hitting him in the head and causing two police officers to come into the room and restrain her.

They were going to send her to the Women's Reformatory in Dire, Indiana, but because of her family's reputation and money she got released into her parents' custody and was driven to the Dean Family home. The next morning brought rain clouds and Dorothy telling her mother that she wanted to 'get some rest' at the Institute near the town of Vesanus, in Illinois, because she wanted to be near the pretty trees. Mildred Dean told her daughter that the family would look after Rebeca while she 'got better' , and by the time the midafternoon rain started falling, a car pulled up to the house with a woman and two men getting out to come get Dorothy. While walking to the car and brushing her hair, she turned and said to her mother to tell Rebeca that she loved her, then looked at the two black men walking to the car besides her and asked them how she looked. Dorothy got into the car and lit a cigarette, then asked the stiff collared, black suit wearing woman that looked like she had been 'weaned' on a pickle for most of her life, where they were driving too? The stiff collared, black suit wearing woman told Dorothy that they were going to take her to a place to 'get better,' then asked Dorothy who Barbara Stanwyck was? Dorothy was taken to the Heinrich Behavioral Institute in Illinois, which was a very reclusive building made of white concrete and marble, and shrouded on a hill by the pretty trees of Oak, Ash, and Sassafras, near the town of Vesanus.

Part VII
An old country saying.

Everyone has to pay for what they've done in the past, and that holds true for many parts of the 'anas' and the rest of society. There was a long standing story throughout the 'anas' and parts farther away, about a black man that killed his former slave owner after he had searched for him for many years. The boy was a slave and had a mother, with brothers and sisters and a father, but the slave owner was terrible to them. The slave owner had his father lynched and beat and sold some of his brothers and sisters, and treated his mother like an animal. The boy grew up to be a man and made a living in society working on a steamship that traveled up and down the rivers. One day he got off the steamship and walked 100 miles to the residence of his former slave owner and when he got there, he killed his former slave owner and those involved with what happened to his family, then walked back to the steamship, never to be seen again. Folks throughout the years, especially farmers and people with livestock, referred to the story as 'the chickens coming home to roost,' or bad coming upon you for the bad you've done in the past.

Dorothy's impulsive behavior carried over at the Heinrich Behavioral Institute, with fights and arguments with the nurses and some patients, causing the clinic to administer shock treatment therapy to settle her moods. After extensive behavioral therapy, Dorothy was released in the fall of 1963 under the supervision of her mother to resume her 'normal' responsibilities of being a wife and mother. With her high I.Q. kicking in, Dorothy began to resume daily life by taking Rebeca to Aurora Middle school and trying to be loving, but distant with Tyrus when he was at home. A windy night at Dorothy's house had her with Rebeca and Abigail 'Sue' Burd eating a large spaghetti dinner and watching the evening news, when the news was interrupted about the execution of Garrett Lee Folsom. The news reported how Garrett Lee Folsom, aged 42, had spent his whole life doing bad things to people since he was 12 years of age, and may have committed his first murder when he was 15 years old. As the three of them watched and listened to the news, it told of how at the age of thirty-seven Garrett Lee Folsom killed 2 men with a hunting knife and had raped and killed 3 young women, both in the towns of Insanus and Versanus in the state of Illinois. Dorothy told

Rebeca and 'Sue' Burd how Garrett Lee Folsom's execution was like an old country saying, that 'the chickens had come home to roost' on his ass, and he had to pay for the bad things he did. Dorothy told Rebeca that she was 'conceived' in the town of Versanus, where the murders happened and where her and Tyrus got married, then casually let Abigail know that she was spending the night over their house. Dorothy didn't feel like driving her to Faulkner County, remembering her last trip there, and with Abigail spending the night, this made Rebeca happy because Abigail already shared half of her room anyway. Rebeca didn't think too much about what her mother had said earlier that night, about her being 'conceived' in the town of Versanus where the 3 girls were killed, until she fell asleep later that night. During the night with the girls fast asleep, Dorothy sat in her bedroom self-medicating on morphine and smoking cigarettes while listening to Patsy Cline songs on the radio. She thought about the killing she did in Missouri and began to think about an old country saying, and wondered when the 'chickens would come home to roost' for her.

The nation was preparing for the Thanksgiving holiday and many people throughout the 'anas' and farther went turkey hunting, while some women went to the grocery stores to buy all the 'fixins' and decorations. Dorothy loved President John F. Kennedy and his wife 'Jackie' for their beautiful youth and vibrant style, with the President being pictured with Hollywood movie stars and entertainers. She had a large presidential picture of him in the living-room and campaigned for him in 1959, which upset a lot of people in the 'anas' that wanted a true Democratic segregationist 'Dixiecrat' president. The 22nd of November was like most bright, breezy days in Indiana, with the exception of Tyrus Van Meter having spent the last few days at home trying to play the dutiful husband and father, while still carrying on an affair with Cheryline Jenkins. Before leaving for work in the morning, Tyrus kissed Dorothy and told her that he loved her like he did back in Missouri and Illinois, and with those words of emotion, they had 'pent up' sex in the kitchen of their house. The children throughout the country were in school getting ready for the holiday season break, and grown folks had bad intentions on their minds.

In the late morning, Dorothy watched on television the arrival of President Kennedy and the First Lady at Love Field in Dallas, Texas, then she drove to a convenience store to pick up some items and noticed some people acting weirdly, thinking they were behaving the way they were because she was around. Dorothy went into a food store to get some supplies, when she heard someone yell in a loud voice in the poultry section, "The President's been shot!". Dorothy drove home and watched the events unfolding on the television, as children were sent home to pray for a wounded President. When Dorothy, Rebeca and Abigail 'Sue' Burd gathered into Dorothy's house in Fairmont to watch on television what was happening to the young President of the United States, by the midday dusk settling upon Indiana, the young President was dead. Afterwards, a young black Muslim preacher that grew up in Omaha, Nebraska was asked what he thought of the assassination of President Kennedy, and having grown up on the farmlands with livestock, he said, "There's an old country saying, that the chickens have come home to roost! And the bad that happened to John F. Kennedy was the result of the bad things that he did in the past!"

The young Black Muslim was exiled from his organization, but not from his faith, and a year later the 'chickens had come home to roost' for him, being shot and killed in front of his wife and children for the bad things he had done in the past. After the assassinations of two prominent people because of their past transgressions, Dorothy became more reclusive and stayed close to her home in Fairmont, occasionally meeting a tall, light colored black woman named Dahlia Black Rollins who took out the trash on occasion in the large backfield yard, that was separated only by a thin wired fence. It was a hot summer day throughout the 'anas' and Dorothy was sitting in the back of her yard with Rebeca, trying to stay cool under the shade of a Maple tree, when Rebeca saw Becky coming out the back of her house, all six-foot, two-inches of her with her mother Dahlia right behind her. They looked and glanced at each other for a while, baking under the hot Indiana sun, when Dorothy got up and yelled, "To hell with this fucking heat, let's all go to the beach and cool down!" Dahlia and Becky stared at the white woman known to be impulsive, when Dorothy took Rebeca in the house abruptly. Within half an hour, Dorothy and Rebeca were in the front of Dahlia's house on Clairmont Street, beeping the horn of her black Ford truck for them to get into the car to go to the beach. Dahlia stood in the doorway of her house, too stunned to move, when Becky ran out of the door and Rebeca got out of the car and they greeted each other like old friends, with the only problems being the staring eyes of people on opposite sides of the thin wired fence. With Dahlia, Becky and her daughter in the black Ford truck, Dorothy Ann Dean Van Meter drove

75 miles outside of town to a large area of secluded land, where black people, white strangers that most had seen before, and sun baked Indians that kept their distance, but waded and swam in Lake Repentance. Dorothy gravitated to Dahlia Black Rollins instantly because of her laid back demeanor, as they sat on lounge chairs watching the tides roll onto the sands off of Lake Repentance. With her tall, lanky body, Becky Black Rollins waded and held Rebeca above the high tides of the lake, as Rebeca was shorter but tough against the currents. When the cooling down of a hot summer day was coming to an end, and the dusk began to set on the realities of life in segregated America, Dahlia asked Dorothy 'why' she drove her and her daughter 75 miles to a lake to go swimming? Dorothy told her sternly, "Water, and the things that live in them don't give a 'shit' what color you are, and sharks don't have conflicts about white or dark meat, they just tear you to pieces!"

Part VIII
Just like Frances Farmer.

Dorothy Ann Dean Van Meter always fancied herself as a Hollywood movie star, and with the deaths of her cousin 'Jimmy' and the young President Kennedy that knew movie stars, her hopes of becoming an actress like her alter-ego, Barbara Stanwyck, faded away in despair. After swimming in Lake Repentance on that hot summer day, Becky and Rebeca only saw each other sparingly when they took out the trash and had brief conversations, mostly about Rebeca's mother not feeling well. When Tyrus did come home to play husband and father, Dorothy would have outright screaming matches with him for all the 'anas' to hear, telling him to go back to that 'Hillbilly whore' that he's been sleeping with! Tyrus told Dorothy on a couple of occasions while leaving the house in anger, that if it wasn't for Rebeca and not wanting to be 'pig fertilizer,' he would never come around her, too which, Dorothy responded by pulling out her gun from her purse and taking a shot at Tyrus, nearly missing his head.

When she wasn't suffering from depression caused by her chronic schizophrenia, and being in her room for days with the curtains drawn to keep out the light, she had screaming arguments with people when she went out to do simple chores, like grocery shopping or getting some wine and cigarettes from the local store. The townsfolk throughout the 'anas' began to talk about something being done about Dorothy's impulsive, violent outbursts, saying amongst themselves that she was 'Just like Frances Farmer,' the beautiful actress of the 1930's and 40's that was declared 'insane' in 1944 and lobotomized in 1950. The rumors got to Mildred Dean, who did not want to see her daughter institutionalized again, and dispelled the rumors by telling certain people that Dorothy would be fine. The young high school girl Abigail 'Sue' Burd still came by to watch Rebeca, but not as much, as Dorothy's behavior became more erratic and unpredictable, even when she would offer 'Sue' Burd $100 dollars to babysit Rebeca, who was now around 12 years of age. A mild spring evening in May had Abigail babysitting, or just hanging out with Rebeca, when Dorothy said she was going out for a couple of hours to 'clear her head,' which Abigail and Rebeca knew to be trouble. Dorothy got in her truck and drove to the 'outskirts' of Fairmont to Sin City, a town run by Chinese gangsters and unscrupulous people from the 'anas' that did all their 'dirty laundry' in the town. Dorothy went to The Han, which was a large bar and gambling place where all vices were accommodated, and walked around as if she owned the place, to the dismay of the owner of The Han. When Dorothy became intoxicated and belligerent, the Chinese woman that ran The Han came over to Dorothy and asked her to leave, and when Dorothy refused, the Chinese woman grabbed Dorothy by the arm and Dorothy pulled away from her, grabbing her gun from her purse and calling her a 'Chinese whore,' then shooting a man in the chest that tried to take the gun away from her.

    Dorothy was arrested for attempted murder and stayed at the police station in the town of Ineffable, where she was to appear in court the next day. In court the next morning, Dorothy's mother appeared in court talking to a lawyer and the judge and when the charges and past arrests were read in the courtroom, Mildred Dean signed a paper declaring her daughter 'insane' and sending her to the Heinrich Behavioral Institute for psychiatric evaluations. When the gavel was struck by the judge, Dorothy was led away through a side door while glancing at her tearful mother, as some in the courtroom talked amongst themselves about what happened to Dorothy Ann Dean Van Meter, saying it was 'Just like Frances Farmer,' then left the courtroom with a sense of relief. The court also issued a warning to Tyrus Van Meter, about being a more 'present' father in Rebeca's life.

Chapter IV
Ling, the Girl from Mount Song

The Han was a well-run and organized gambling establishment that served the vices of the hypocrites throughout the 'anas,' and those of the people that traveled many distances to Sin City. The Han was run by the Chinese mafia and had business interests throughout the midwest and extending as far as Canada, with the unknown 'boss' called Ling. It was said in many places that Ling rose to power by forming alliances with different Clans, then having all the male 'bosses' killed and becoming the 'Chi-zi,' or leader.

Ling was known from the people that came over with her, many of them being 'elders' of the Clans, of how she survived many battles with the Japanese and was a ruthless child fighter. To escape Japanese atrocities from the wars around them, the people of her village lived in the cliffs of Mount Song, along the southern bank of the Yellow River, and would commit raids on Japanese military posts around the islands of Mount Song. They were called 'phantoms from the cliffs' because they could disappear into the water at night, and the water remained still, not finding any of them with searches well into the morning. She learned to dive off the cliffs of Mount Song every morning into the Yellow River, to catch fish and other sea creatures, and learned how to walk like a mountain cat on the cliffs to hunt for the animals that lived in Mount Song. The 'elders' taught her the art of torture for captured Japanese soldiers, telling her that they would have done worse to her if she were captured. The Americans defeated Japan, officially ending World War II and liberating islands that had been brutalized by the Land of the Rising Sun, with some of them being the islands along the Yellow River. The warlord leader of Mount Song was Ito 'Sonny' Kwan, and he took the young Ling as a wife, knowing of her skills for survival and cunning. Ito 'Sonny' Kwan was the most powerful and ruthless of the warlord leaders along the vast Yellow River, which included four other mountains in China. The American Navy gathered the people from the Five Great Mountains and because they helped fight the Japanese in the

War, they sailed them across the Pacific Ocean and onto the West Coast, then being transported through Canada and into the midwest, sprinkling the people from the islands along the way. The United States Government gave each of the Five Great Mountain leaders and their people a million dollars per island, and some supposedly worthless land in Canada and the midwest for their efforts.

The culture they came from had existed for thousands of years and invented the modern day mafia, and the leaders of each Clan from the Five Great Mountains formed the Hei Shou-dang Mafia. They took the money and land given to them by the government to get neutralization and diplomatic immunity, along with building permits and gambling licenses. The Hei-Shou-dang Mafia was involved in the trades of prostitution and the importing and selling of heroin, along with owning opium dens and Chinese restaurants in most midwestern towns. Ito 'Sonny' Kwan was a well-built man of six-feet, two inches tall and weighing a solid 225 pounds, with strikingly handsome features and long black hair that matched the intensity of his black eyes. With cunning, intelligence, and being more ruthless than the other leaders of the four mountain clans, at age thirty-five, Ito became the 'Chi-zi,' or leader, of the Hei-Shou-dang Mafia. Ling learned the ways of the Hei-Shou-dang as she remained loyal to Ito, even personally killing some people thought to be conspirators against him, while forming alliances because of her powerful position as the wife of the Chi-zi. During the times of Ito's reign as leader of the Hei-Shou-dang Mafia, it prospered the other members of the Five Great Mountain Clans with their investments in gambling and drugs, and the constant need for American vices being met in the mid-1950's and 60's. Ling was a young wife with ambitions of her own, but Ito continued to treat her more like a teenage girl needing discipline than what she had really become, a cunning rival.

Part I
The Five Great Mountains along the Yellow River and the Hei-Shou-dang Mafia.

In modern America, the Mafia had five 'bosses' of the Five Families within the five boroughs of New York, but the Hei-Shou-dang had been doing it for centuries. Along the vast Yellow River that flows throughout China are five islands, each one of them formed by a large mountain and having a 'Chi-zi' leader. The leaders of the islands often had wars against each other but mostly fought the Japanese, and raided other islands around their territories. The Five Mountain Clans that made up the Hei-Shou-dang Mafia were **The Tai Shan Clan**, meaning *tranquil*, **The Hua Shan Clan,** meaning *splendid,* **The Heng Shan Clan**, from the Hunan province of China, meaning *balancing*, and another **Heng Shan Clan,** but from the province of Shanxi meaning *permanent*, and finally **The Song Shan Clan**, meaning *lofty.*

    They brought their ways and traditions with them to America, but were not the first of their kind to arrive in North America, as they now had connections around the world. The **Song Shan Clan** from Mount Song was the most powerful of the five clans and Ito 'Sonny' Kwan was a third generation leader, learning the ways of being a 'Chi-zi' since he was a child. Ling's mother was a wise and skilled woman, with exceptional beauty and the ability to dive into the Yellow River and stay under for minutes at a time. Her father was a respected man throughout the other four clans and was known for his ruthless skills for killing, along with a keen mind for sabotage and defeating the Japanese. Ling's father had aspirations of being the 'Chi-zi' leader of the Song Shan Clan and when these aspirations were revealed, he was killed while serving an 'elder' of the clan, with some believing that Ito had something to do with his death.

Part II
Et tu, Ling?

The heads of the Five Clans and their many associates met in a small town in Canada known as Orr Pass, to discuss the many interests of the Hei-Shou-dang Mafia. The wives of the 'bosses' stayed behind in their respective territories while the 'bosses' brought their concubines along with them, giving Ling time to plot her plan of becoming the Chi-zi. She started by gathering the wives of the 4 other crime bosses in a small town in San Francisco called Betrail, then told them how their husbands, the 'bosses,' treated them like pigs and had more respect for their concubines. After much discussion and debate, Ling convinced the wives of the Hei-Shou-dang to have their loyal concubines kill their husbands, therefore making the women the leaders of the Hei-Shou-dang Mafia. Within months after the gathering of the 'bosses' of the Hei-Shou-dang in Canada, they were all being killed either by assassination or poisoning by their loyal concubines, except for Ito

'Sonny' Kwan. Ling planted a venomous snake in the house she shared with Ito and spent days with him, assuring him of her loyalty and that she had nothing to do with the deaths of the leaders of the Hei-Shou-dang. On a windy day on the outskirts of Indiana where they shared a modest styled Chinese decorated house, Ito was praying in the livingroom when he was bit by the snake Ling had planted, and within seconds the poisonous venom was taking hold of Ito. Ling came out of the bedroom as Ito struggled with the poison, then saying to her;

"Et tu, Ling? I knew this day was coming ever since our days on the cliffs of Mount Song, when I killed your father because he wanted to be the leader of the Song Clan!"

"I know you killed my father because he challenged your inheritance to be the leader of the Song Clan, but I plotted my revenge against you and others years ago, by listening to my mother while fishing off the cliffs of Mount Song."

"Your mother was a very beautiful woman, as you turned out to be, Ling."

"Yes, she was, and may you have peace with our ancestors when you die, Ito."

"I have had many enemies during my lifetime and I married you for your cunning and beauty. You were always loyal to me and killed some of my betrayers, but like Brutus was with Cesar in the end, Et tu, Ling, et tu?"

After the death of Ito 'Sonny' Kwan, the most powerful leader of the Hei-Shou-dang Mafia, Ling became the Chi-zi with the approval of the wives of the slain bosses. The girl from the cliffs of Mount Song was now the head of the most powerful Chinese crime organization in the midwest, and parts farther than the cornfields around them.

Part III
The 'Id' of Thaddeus Baker.

Most of the police officers throughout the 'anas' were racist and corrupt, and used their authority to keep other races in their 'places' and satisfy their vices as they pleased. The white police officers in most towns had cousins or relatives that were either sheriffs in other towns, politicians in different states or judges in other districts, and violated the laws they were supposed to uphold and protect. Many of them had wives and children and went to church on Sunday's, but would slap their wives around and kick the family dog during the week, then visit their Chinese girlfriends on Friday nights. In public they praised their wives as the most precious of God's creations, but behind closed doors they treated their wives like dirt farmers and wouldn't hesitate to kill a black man if it was even mentioned that he had looked at a white woman.

Thaddeus Baker was a police officer from one of the 'ana' towns called Ineffable and was like most of his fellow officers, racist and corrupt and always trying to satisfy his vices. He was a diminutive man of five-feet, four-inches with sandy brown hair and brown eyes, but always tried to overcompensate his lack of height by being an overzealous loud-mouth and verbal bully. Thaddeus came from a long line of policemen and had ancestors that fought wars for America dating back to the Civil War, and never failed to remind people of his lineage when he confronted them. He was raised to hate just about every race on the planet and as a young man he did just that, by hating the black and brown skinned people, the Japanese and the Jews, and most of the Chinese because they looked Japanese, but this didn't stop him from going to The Han. When Thaddeus went to The Han in Sin City with some of his cop friends on Friday nights, he acted like a 'Napoleonic tyrant' by having drinks and not paying for them and talking to the workers of The Han as if they were a lower class of people. He had sex with Chinese prostitutes and paid them by throwing money on the floor for them to pick up, never paying them the full amount of their services, and threatened to arrest or deport any 'yellow bastard' that slighted him.

A mild April evening had Thaddeus Baker and his usual crew of cop friends at The Han, exploiting and satisfying their vices when Thaddeus felt disrespected by a Chinese worker and slapped her, not knowing it was Ling. There were two men and a woman that approached Thaddeus with bad intentions but Ling waved them away, and said to Thaddeus, "Your 'Id' or ego will be your downfall, Officer Baker!" Thaddeus responded by spitting in her face and slapping her again, then having his cop friends arrest some of the Chinese workers for suspicious behavior. The workers and Ling were arrested and taken to the police station in the town of Ineffable, and while Thaddeus boasted of his arrest to his fellow officers, Ling and the other workers from The Han were released within four hours. After finding out about their release from the police station, Thaddeus became enraged and swore to his fellow officers that he was going to rid the 'anas' of the 'yellow menace,' when a fellow officer told him, "Thaddeus, an ego left unchecked is a dangerous thing!" Thaddeus ignored the officer's warning and prepared to take his family camping up in Canada, to the family lodge to meet his brother Baron 'Buck' Baker and his family.

Another hot summer began in 1965 and Thaddeus was preparing to take his wife and three children to the Algonquin National Park in Canada, but before leaving the town of Ineffable, Thaddeus told his fellow officers that he would probably return as sheriff of the town and was responsible for the lynching of a black man that supposedly looked at his wife. His fellow police officers and other townsfolk in the town of Ineffable were growing weary of Thaddeus' egotistical attitude, but none of them told him about the Chinese woman he slapped at The Han, or the danger he could be in for the offense.

Thaddeus had a pretty, petite wife named Sylvia and they had three children, Autumn was the oldest at ten years of age, then her sister Summer who was eight years old, and their six year old little brother named Thaddeus, jr. On a Saturday morning in June, Thaddeus got everyone into the family station wagon to begin the 1,890 mile drive to the town of Makepeace where they had a family lodge, looking forward to some seclusion and spending time with his brother.

Part IV
The end of Karma.

After two days and nights of driving and a couple of stops along the way, Thaddeus and his family reached the town of Makepeace and the family lodge, where his brother and his wife and son were awaiting them. Once inside the lodge, the thirty-four year old Thaddeus Baker felt like he had arrived and was a 'lock' to be the next sheriff of Ineffable, immediately telling his younger brother 'Buck' before they even settled in. Baron 'Buck' Baker was four years younger than Thaddeus but seven inches taller, which made Thaddeus even more 'Napoleonic' around his brother. Baron had a pretty, full-sized brunette wife with sultry brown eyes named Tilly, short for Matilda, and a somewhat awkward, shy son named David, whom Thaddeus picked on by calling him a 'sissy' and a fagot. These insults would infuriate Tilly and cause her to go at Thaddeus physically, but he would apologize and all would be forgotten.

They spent their time as the typical American family by going to the

Algonquin National Park to sightsee and fish by the Sloth River, while Thaddeus and his brother drank liquor and their wives' smoked cigarettes and ignored each other. Sometimes Thaddeus would skip a family outing, telling everyone that his back was 'killing' him from all his police work in the town of Ineffable, but was anxious for his family to leave so he could be left alone to feed his morphine addiction and rub a cold bottle of milk across his forehead. When a day of family activities drew to an end with the setting of the Canadian sun, Thaddeus and his brother 'Buck' would get themselves together to go out and do some 'brotherly' bonding. They would drive 25 miles from the town of Makepeace to go to a bar called The Dying Fox where they could get drunk without the wives and children being around, and a place where Thaddeus could brag about his exploits of being a cop in the town of Ineffable. As with most ego's unchecked, Thaddeus brought his ego, or 'Id,' to the town of Makepeace and the Dying Fox bar, where he insulted the mostly Chinese workers and irritated the regulars with his threats and braggadocious talk. An insulted Chinese woman approached him and said, "You have bad karma, Officer Baker, and you should leave this place! Whatever karma you and your family have, it will soon come to an end!" Thaddeus became irate and tried to use his police authority in The Dying Fox to arrest people, with the morphine taking hold of his ego and 'little tyrant' attitude, when his brother grabbed him outside and said he was hungry and wanted to get some Chinese food. Thaddeus and his younger brother laughed hysterically on the gravel pavement of the parking lot in front of the Dying Fox bar, laughing about the irony of abusing Chinese people then wanting Chinese food to bring home to their families.

    The brothers got into Baron's blue Ford truck and drove the ten miles to the town of Plato, where they could get Chinese food at a remote restaurant called The Flying Duck, which was discreetly owned by Ling and the Hei-Shou-dang Mafia. Once inside the restaurant, Thaddeus began his belittling of the Chinese race and encouraged his brother to do the same, but Baron was hesitant to mock the Chinese workers while Thaddeus called him a 'sissy' and a coward. The people working in the restaurant were servile and did not respond to the insults of Thaddeus Baker and his half embarrassed brother, then handed them their Chinese food and bowed to them in gratitude. The brothers got into the truck with the Chinese food and headed to the lodge, knowing the children would enjoy the rare treat and the wives the bottle of wine they had, when Thaddeus began boasting to his brother about being the next sheriff of Ineffable and having a black man strung-up because he made a 'pass' at Sylvia. They were almost at the lodge when Baron pulled the truck over to the side of the road, and told his brother that he was a 'despicable' person and if he ever called his son David a 'sissy' or 'fagot' again, he would punch his lights out and throw him off of a mountain! Thaddeus laughed off his brothers' comments and continued to talk about himself, when Baron said to him as they pulled up to the lodge, "Just like that black man you had lynched, you ended his karma, and your karma will end as a result of it, Thaddeus!'

When they entered the lodge, Sylvia and Tilly had already had a couple of cocktails and suddenly became best friends, while the children played board games and told silly jokes. Everyone stopped what they were doing and put out their plates for the delicious smelling Chinese food, with the kids talking about the food like it had just come from Communist China, and Thaddeus skipping the eating festivities to go to the bathroom and then to the kitchen to make himself a drink. He left the bathroom and walked down the hallway towards the kitchen to make his drink, when he heard loud coughing coming from the living-room and his wife saying, "I think somethings wrong with the food!' Thaddeus went into the dimly lit kitchen and was making his drink, when he heard a familiar voice say, "Good evening, Officer Baker." When Thaddeus squinted his eyes to get a clearer look at who spoke to him, he saw it was Ling Kwan, leader of the Hei-Shou-dang Mafia, with two female assassins dressed in black suits and wearing dark green sunglasses. Before Thaddeus could move a 'Napoleonic' muscle in his body, Ling had her 'female' sword at Thaddeus's throat and told him how pretty his wife Sylvia was, and that she didn't deserve to live with a 'white trash pig' like him! Baron 'Buck' Baker got up from the living-room and went into the kitchen, and when he got there, he saw his brother with a sword being held to his throat by a Chinese woman, and when he made a move towards Ling, the two female assassins executed him with their 'female' swords within seconds. Ling walked Thaddeus out into the living-room to witness his wife and three children, along with Tilly and her son David, slowly die from the poisoned Chinese food they had eaten, then was tied up and bound by the two female assassins without any resistance on his part. The wives clutched their children in agony, as David was the first child to succumb from the poisoning, when Ling walked over to Sylvia and stared at her and her three children, then began stroking Sylvia's blonde hair and telling her that it was her husband's ego that brought this fate upon them. Sylvia spit in her face and told her, "I hope you rot in hell, you 'yellow' bitch!" then slowly died along with her three children, and Tilly.

Thaddeus screamed and begged, asking Ling why she had done this to him and his family? Ling told him, "Officer Baker, most of life revolves around karma, and that 'karma' is the sum of a person's actions in this and previous states of existence. Karma is the deciding fate in future existences, and Officer Baker, you have come to the end of your karma!" Ling and the two female assassins took Thaddeus with them and put him in a car, then set the lodge on fire by making it look like a gas explosion, then drove to the Sloth River. There were no more plans to be the sheriff in the town of Ineffable and his ego was finally 'checked,' as Thaddeus was tortured in the woods by the Sloth River with methods Ling had learned as a girl from the 'elders' of Mount Song. The Sloth River is a long, slow moving river and Thaddeus's body was never found and the death of his family was ruled as an 'accidental homicide,' because of the gas leak that was discovered during the investigation. The unfortunate deaths of Sylvia Baker and her three children, along with Baron 'Buck' Baker and his wife and son, and the mysterious disappearance of Officer Thaddeus Baker was a shock to the people that lived in the town of Ineffable. Mrs. Sylvia Baker was a well-respected school teacher and her children were well liked, but not much sympathy was shown for the loss of Thaddeus Baker. Ling Kwan disappeared and was not heard from or seen for several years, but rumors throughout the 'anas' were that she still ran the Hei-Shou-dang Mafia, but from a distance. Meanwhile, there were other troubles on the horizon for some people in the 'anas,' especially in the town of Sometime.

Chapter V
Ms. Sheila, and the Only People She Ever Loved

Sheila Iris Thompson grew up in the town of Sometime all her life and when she was younger, she was an all-state athlete in basketball and track and field, and got accolades and praise from white people throughout the 'anas' and they promised her many things. As she grew older and those promises not being kept, besides those people that were close to her, she hated everyone in the town of Sometime, and anyone associated with them! She was the youngest child of Xavier and Julia Thompson, who had four other children named Charles, Malcolm, Tyrone and Lydia, and taught their children the importance of God, education, standing up for oneself, and that white people couldn't be trusted. The Thompson's grew up in a big house that was always filled with kids from school, but Sheila preferred to play with a girl her age that lived down the street named Dahlia Black, who was a mischievous girl who liked to go into the woods and pretend they were somewhere else in the world. Both were born a year before the stock market crash which led to the Great Depression, and if times weren't hard enough, they got even harder, as neighbor turned on neighbor and lynchings became a common occurrence. Dahlia's mother was Wanda Parker Black and was a full-blooded Iriquos Indian, and very resourceful about living on the things around her and hunting animals in the mountains of Indiana, for food in the lean times. There were times when she would go hunting on horseback into the woods, with her rifle and hunting knives and come across a negro hanging from a tree. Wanda Parker Black would climb the tree and cut the negroe down and bury them, putting their souls to rest as her culture had taught her. These mysterious acts, instead of letting the animals in the woods do the 'cleaning up' of a hung body, gave Wanda the nickname throughout the 'anas' as 'the Soul keeper' because she kept the hung people's souls alive by cutting them down, and then burying them in a decent, Christian way.

Sheila's father, Xavier Thompson, was an engineer at a large manufacturing plant and a follower of the teachings of Marcus Garvey, which nearly got him hung or killed on many occasions, and her mother Julia was a God fearing 'domestic' for white people and their children. She briefly worked as a domestic house servant for the Dean family in Sometime and remembered how the depression wasn't affecting them much, but how they had a hard time controlling their daughter Dorothy because of her impulsive behavior, but how the 'crazy little white girl' took a shine to her. There was an ancient saying told by those who could remember it, that "Tragedy brings change, and change, hopefully, brings about peace," and that saying became true with the tragedy of World War II and the lifting of the heavy fog of The Great Depression, and changing the country from a backwoods nation to a world power!

The war brought change and tragedy to the Thompson family as Mrs. Julia Thompson was dying of cancer, and her older children were gradually leaving the house to seek their own ways in the world. Sheila's older sister Lydia stayed on with the family, promising Sheila that she wouldn't leave her side and would help her with their dying mother, but when a midwestern breeze of a good man blew Lydia's way, she left Sheila behind to deal with the island of 'Now what?'

Part I
The children of War.

The children of the world are always the casualties of war, having to change their joyous childhoods into hardened existences because of the evils of a few grown people. The country was getting back to a sense of normality after The Great Depression, and started flexing and boasting its might around the world until some disrespected Japanese with planes ended American soldiers having sex with girls in Hawaii, blowing them to 'smithereens' and ending the countries tranquility in the world. A year after FDR declared war on Japan, Sheila was about to start school at Sonoma High when her mother died from her painful bout with cancer, leaving her to live alone with her father and the occasional visits from her sister Lydia. With another crisis to deal with that the country got itself into, Sheila became a resourceful girl by working at a grocery store and knowing how to hustle a few dollars, a trait that she learned from her criminal brother Malcolm. Dahlia learned ways of survival from her mother and aunt Mildred but at an early age, had a desire to go to Egypt and Italy from the books she read and leave the town of

Sometime forever.

Sheila and Dahlia were best friends when they started Sonoma High School in 1942, having known each other since they were kids, with the bigger Sheila being the protector and Dahlia the pretty troublemaker. With all the children in the country going back to school during the war it affected them differently, as everyone in the country had to ration and some people didn't have anything to ration at all. If they were fortunate enough to go to the Saturday matinee and see a movie picture show, the intermissions showed scenes of the War around the world and the sufferings of children caused by it. The dirty, half-starved kids on the screen were called 'The children of War' because they had to survive the climate of war, and would never be children again! They talked about going to high school together and how Sheila was relieved that her mother died, telling Dahlia that she didn't have to suffer anymore and how after seeing the movies, they were now children of war!

Part II
Inner circle.

Sheila and Dahlia were now attending Sonoma High School together and stuck close like magnets, only separating when the other had a different class. She was already a well-proportioned girl at six feet, three inches and weighing about 165 pounds, with beautiful dark features and a black afro that matched her naive eyes and liked to laugh at silly jokes. Dahlia, on the other hand, was a half black, half Iriquos Indian and was skeptical of many people, telling Sheila not to get too close to people and to keep an 'inner circle' between them and to keep the rest of them out! Dahlia LeeAnn Black was perhaps the prettiest girl in school, with long black kinky hair that extended almost the length of her five feet, five inches of brashness, and a skin tone that matched the Arizona desert. One day when the pledge of allegiance was sworn by the right hand over the heart to God for loyalty to the country, Dahlia saw Sheila talking to a girl after class and walked over to them, clutching her books in her hands and arms as if she had been betrayed! When Dahlia got to the two of them talking, Dahlia asked the short, cunning black girl why she was talking to Sheila, and before the girl could say anything, Dahlia slapped her into the girls' lockers and told her to stay away from Sheila!

Again, basketball and sports were a staple of midwestern life regardless of the war, and the athletic abilities of Sheila and Dahlia did not exclude them, as they did well in sports and met boys from other schools. The both of them were at a basketball game cheering on Sonoma High School against its rival, Lincoln High School, when the star player on the team from Lincoln High School approached Dahlia and told her that he would go out with her after he beats Sonoma! She dismissed his arrogance until she watched him dismantle her home team, then became enthralled with the senior from Lincoln High School named James Rollins. He was a good looking black man of nineteen years of age and was one of the best high school players in the country, with Dahlia already having her eyes set on the six foot, five inch tall basketball star of a rival school.

Dahlia courted James and even had Sheila beat up a girl from Lincoln High School, all because the girl was wearing James' varsity sweater at practice, causing most of the girls from both schools to be weary of Dahlia's Iroquois ways . It was only a matter of time when the tall, imposing James Rollins wilted like a June flower under the sun, and succumbed to Dahlia's aggressive ways, adding to the fact that she was a most beautiful girl. Throughout time, everyone has met someone in order to meet someone else, and such was the case when James Rollins introduced his best friend named Joe Payton to Sheila Thompson. She immediately took to the awkward, half illiterate Joe Payton, whom some said was as 'bright as a cloudy day,' but was a very large young man at six feet and seven inches tall to a pine tree, and nearly weighing as much. Regardless of his intellect, Joe Payton was the best defensive football player at his age in the country and a lot of people made promises to him, as most of them did with James and the rest of Sheila's inner circle. In the year of 1942 as the war went on, a black man was the heavyweight champion of the world and black men began 'puffing' their chests out a little bit more than usual, but mindful not to do it around white folks, as the 'inner circle' between Sheila and Joe Payton, his best friend James and Dahlia became closer.

Although they were young, they grew up fast because of the War and learned how to 'fend' for themselves at an early age. The four of them were together all the time with some school kids calling them 'The gang,' and that they only let a select few into their inner circle of trust, as Dahlia almost trusted no one, even those closest to her. They went to school socials and danced to the music of Duke Ellington and other jazz musicians of the day, when a young man from Lincoln High School told Dahlia that she looked like Billie Holiday the jazz singer and got aggressive to dance with her, when James came over and punched the kids lights out, thus, ending their night of social activities but reaffirming their bond to each other.

As the seasons change, so do the lives of people, and the lives of James and Joe 'Big Joe' Payton were about to change as they were graduating from high school, and facing the prospects of a real world. Sheila Thompson and Dahlia Black were only sophomores in high school, but ready to get ahead of themselves by joining James and Joe on their endeavors into the 'grown world,' when they told them to finish school and that nothing would change, regardless of what they decided. What James and Joe decided was to go to Lincoln State University on athletic scholarships, promising Dahlia and Sheila that they would stay loyal to them, and that it was better than joining the Army! On a fall day as the leaves were beginning to turn colors, James, Joe, Dahlia, and Sheila said their good-byes as the boys went off to college together, promising the girls 'big things in college and to visit every chance they got. During the emotional departure, Dahlia was not as emotional as the others, thinking how she loved James but if she never saw him again, life goes on, while Sheila was crying and telling James and Joe to be careful and besides her mother and Dahlia, they were the only people she ever loved!

Part III
An offer from Chicago you can't refuse!

The university that James and Joe went to was not the university they saw and were promised in the brochure, being nothing more than a dry patch of land with false promises, like the book *The Grapes of Wrath* by John Steinbeck, and they immediately became disillusioned with their surroundings. The tall, athletic James Rollins was a good athlete in basketball and baseball, with an ability for track and field, while Joe could hit a baseball out of the cornfields, but preferred to take his pent up emotions on the dry patch of dirt that was their football field. They were star athletes for 'the patch of dirt university' and to make matters worse, they were just as broke as the dirt around them. Their prowess did not go unrecognized when a clean-cut black man approached them, asking them to come to Chicago and play semi-pro ball for money. The boys from the town of Sometime had been clawing away at Lincoln University for two years, watching others make money off of their talents and getting nothing, and were interested in hearing what the clean-cut man from Chicago had to say? They met the man off campus in a dingy restaurant, with James helping Big Joe with his stuttering problem so they wouldn't make fools of themselves with the slick man from Chicago.

"Good afternoon, gentlemen, my name is Demitrius Lassiter and I'm here on the behalf of Mr. Walcott from Chicago. You two are fine young men, and Mr. Walcott is interested in you playing for his 'interests' in Chicago?"

"Wa, Wa, What types of interests, Mr. Fancy man?"

"Joe, shut the fuck up and stop stuttering! You'll have to excuse my friend's nervousness, we come from the town of Sometime and don't venture out much, except to play sports!"

"Not a problem, I spent time in a place not too far from Sometime, in a place called Dire, ever heard of it?"

"Th, Th, That's where they send the bad people, right Mr. Lassiter?"

"Some people! Anyway, Mr. Walcott is willing to pay the both of you ten thousand dollars a year to play for his baseball and football 'interests,' providing you do certain 'things' for Mr. Walcott."

"Mr. Lassiter, I came to this god forsaken university on an athletic scholarship, along with my best friend Joe and would very much like to get out of this patch of dirt, what can we expect from you?"

"Here's two hundred dollars, apiece!"

"La, La, Lawd have mercy, I ain't seen this kind of money 'cept' for banks and criminal peoples! What ya thinkin, James?"

"What if we say no, Mr. Lassiter?"

"James Rollins, you look like a smart young man, and I didn't come all the way from Chicago to negotiate with some young fucking nigger hayseeds! I'm here to tell both of you that you've been made an offer from Chicago you can't refuse, so get your little belongings and let's go, there's a car outside waiting to take the both of you to Chicago!"

'Ya, Ya, Ya means the big city, Ch, Ch, "Checargo," Mr. La, Lassat, her?"

"You're a big boy, but not that sharp! Stay close to your lanky friend James, he seems to know how to handle himself, besides, you're not smart enough to deal with Chicago!"

Later in the evening, after they got their meager possessions together and told no one from their school where they were going, James and Joe Payton got on a Greyhound bus with tickets given to them from 'the slick man' from Chicago. When they got on the shiny silver bus, Joe Payton was nervous about leaving his familiar surroundings, with James reassuring him that everything would be alright when they got to Illinois and easing his fears, knowing that his large friend was gullible to people, but if provoked, Joe could choke a person to death in less time it takes to make a pot of coffee. They got off in the town of Calumet and met Demitrius Lassiter, who drove them to the Lincoln Cafe and told them that they would be meeting Mr. Walcott later. Before Joe could stutter a word from his gullible mouth, James told him to 'shut the fuck up' until Mr. Lassiter finishes telling them who this Mr. Walcott 'fella' was? He told them that Mr. Walcott 'ran' things for the black people in town, and that their athletic abilities would be of great use to Mr. Walcott. The drive to the cafe was fascinating for Joe Payton as he looked at the lights from some large buildings, and black people walking around wearing fancy clothes, not the dirt farmer overalls he was accustomed to seeing people wear every day, when he said to James that Illinois looked like a pretty fast town, when James told him that Illinois is a state, not a town!

They got to the Lincoln cafe and were told to sit at a table and order something to eat, because Mr. Walcott was coming from the racetrack and would be about an hour getting to the cafe. He sat down with the boys and had a cup of coffee when James asked him what kind of 'fella' Mr. Walcott is, when Demitrius Lassitter told him that Mr. Walcott used to be a prizefighter and was pretty good, until he did a stint in Sing Sing State Prison for beating two men to death but got out early for good behavior, and settled in Calumet. He told them that Mr. Walcott was a nice man, but not one to be 'fucked with' and to always be polite around him because he respected manners, and that manners could get you a long way in life. As Joe was busy looking around at the well-dressed black people walking by, Demetrius was talking to James about some of the things that go on in Calumet, while James could only think to himself, 'What the fuck did we get into'?

"M, M, Mista Lassiter, w,w,what' happenz' to people that'z rude with M,M, Mista Walcotts?"

"Joe, we don't hang black folks around here like they do where you're from, but if you get out of line with Mr. Walcott, people have a way of not being seen anymore!"

"Mr. Lassitter, what kind of 'deal' is Mr. Walcott proposing to us?"

"Listen, both of you hayseeds are going to get an offer from Chicago you can't refuse! Anyway, do you want to go back to that patch of dirt school and be broke all the time?"

"I, I, I'z tired of being broke Mr. L, L, Lassita, and I like to eat! Those people at the college p,p,promised me and James' things, not near one of them p,p,promises come true!"

"Well, young man, if you and James listen to Mr. Walcott you won't have the problem of being broke, besides, you probably have a girlfriend that you'd like to do nice things for, right?"

"H, H, How did you know I had a girl, her name is Sheila Thompson and I, I, I'z gonna marry her when she gets out of school, M, M, Mr. Lassita!"

"That sounds admirable, try not to get yourself killed in the process big boy, Calumet can be rough!"

They continued to talk at the table about the offer from Chicago that they couldn't refuse, with James periodically telling Joe to 'shut the fuck up' and stop stuttering with a mouth full of food, when a tall, well-dressed man walked into the cafe, causing some to look up from their meal and others to exist the backdoor. He was about six-two and looked well-built from under his coat and when he took his gray Fedora hat off and smiled, it revealed a smooth skinned black man with graying black hair and a scar over his left eye and a gold cap over his front tooth. Mr. Walcott sat down next to Demitrius and looked at the fully grown, slacked jawed yokels from the town of Sometime and smiled, then told them to close their mouths and to sit up straight when he was talking to them, so there wouldn't be any misunderstandings!

Mr. Walcott told the boys that he had many business interests, most of them not involving kids or teenagers, but had interests in semi-professional sports like basketball, baseball and football. Mr. Walcott made them an offer to play semi-professional sports for his Chicago interests and in return, he would pay them fifty dollars a week and their traveling expenses. They looked at each other, mouths agape and eyes wide open, as if they had made the big time and accepted the offer from Mr. Walcott that they couldn't refuse. Mr. Walcottt smiled at them with his gold front tooth shining brighter when the sun reached it, and told them that Demetrius would handle the paperwork and to write to loved one's because they would be gone for a while. He finished his cup of coffee and told James and Joe that they would be staying at the Calumet Inn, not far from where they were dining and that Demetrius would be keeping an eye on them so they didn't get into any trouble, or have thoughts about leaving town to a patch of dirt to see their girlfriends with money in their pockets! Before leaving the cafe and people straining their necks or eyeballs to see if he was still there, Mr. Walcott told the boys that proper manners and honesty were a staple of his character, and if disrespected or violated, Dire, Indiana would seem like a resort to them, and that there was nothing after Dire!

The two twenty year young hicks from the town of Sometime got settled into the Calumet Inn, enjoying the bottle of 'ripple wine' that Demetrious gave to them along with one hundred dollars, of which James kept eighty, knowing Joe's gullibility and lack of responsibility in such matters of money, and as they celebrated their new found fortune they began writing letters to Dahlia and Sheila about their success in Illinois, looking towards the future like grown people. Within a week of getting acclimated with the town of Calumet and the other players from the semi-professional teams, James Rollins quickly established himself as an excellent left-handed pitcher and basketball player, while Joe 'Big Joe' Payton dominated the negro football league as a defensive lineman, causing the opposing teams to have an ambulance on the ready every time he played against them and could hit a baseball a country mile. The seasons dictate sports and the time spent away from those you love, and such was the case between James, Dahlia, Joe and Sheila, as the boys sent them money from Illinois and visited them as often as possible, reaffirming to the sophomores at Sonoma High School that when they graduated they were going to be married and start families like grown people someday, as long as they listened to Mr. Walcott and saved up enough money to leave the town of Sometime, forever!

Part IV
Becoming Ms. Sheila.

The War continued to drag on for the country until FDR died while President of the United States, and with the impatience of certain white people in Washington against the stubbornness of Japan, they dropped atomic bombs on their country to wipe them off the face of the earth, or at least plunge *'The Land of the Rising Sun'* into the depths of the oceans. When the dictator of Germany blew his brains out in a bunker with his wife, there was a sense of renewal in the American spirit for winning the War, but not for those of a different skin color regardless of their achievements at home. It was now two years past since the last leaves of corn blew through the midwestern plains, when Sheila and Dahlia were coming into their own as third year students at Sonoma Valley College, inserting their natural beauty, size, determination, and outright dislike for other people not of their 'inner circle' to their advantage. They were both outstanding athletes in school and got All-State Honors again, with articles written about them in local newspapers about their athletic prowess.

The boys had accepted Mr. Walcott's offer and were now playing semi-pro baseball and football, depending on the season, and went back to Sometime to see Sheila and Dahlia, taking them to the movies and *'Lindy Hop'* dances in school gymnasiums and dancehalls. Their 'inner circle' rules regarding other people was beginning to break, as the good looking, tall James Rollins began talking to other people, not all of them men, as Dahlia was more concerned about going to a faraway country and leaving the dirt patches of Sometime! Sheila and Joe didn't have those problems as they only wanted to be with each other, with Joe Payton telling Sheila that he was going to marry her when she finishes school, which took him fifteen minutes because of his stuttering. When the boys got back to the town of Calumet, 'Big' Joe Payton was warned by Demitrius Lassitter about money he borrowed and had not paid on, with James promising Demitrius that the borrowed money would be paid, as Joe looked around at the lights of Calumet, oblivious to the conversation next to him.

It was the summer vacation from schools around the country and as the students parted ways, Sheila Thompson decided to spend some time with her sister Lydia and her husband Daniel, along with their two children in the town of Shiloh. Dahlia Black decided to spend her time with her mother Wanda Parker Black, anxious to learn things from her that the teachers never taught at Sonoma Valley College. The town of Shiloh was known for being a hostile place towards black people, with most of the white people in authority being members of the Klu Klux Klan, but momentarily suspending their hatred because of the 'feel good' nature of the country after the war and that blacks had actually contributed to the victory for the country. The summer in the town of Shiloh brought excessive heat and the attitudes of constantly sweating people, when Sheila left her aggravating sister's house and went to the local store to get some ice cream and fruit. When she went into the store, hot and not familiar with her surroundings, Sheila accidentally walked into a 'White Only' store and browsed around looking for what she wanted, when a white woman saw her and threw some bananas at her and calling her a 'nigger monkey' and to leave the store. Although she was in the town of Shiloh, Sheila knew her place in society and tried to ignore the boney, pale white, brown haired woman who looked like she had been 'weaned' on something bitter growing up, when the woman walked over to Sheila and spit in her face, then slapping her and telling her to get out of the store, again! Turning the other cheek was not something that Sheila Thompson took from the Bible, slapping the white woman into another aisle and causing her to yell for help in the store because a 'Nigger woman was trying to kill her,' when two white men intervened! The two intoxicated white men followed Sheila out into the parking lot of the store and began harassing her, when one of them said, "Hey, nigger woman, you can't just go around slapping decent white folks, there's penalties for that!"

She tried to walk away when one of the men grabbed her by the arm, causing her to yell out, "Get your damn hands off of me," and punched the white man in the face!

The two men regrouped and began to manhandle Sheila in the parking lot, as some of the people from the 'White Only' store watched the attack or just pushed their shopping carts with their children to their cars, ignoring what was happening to the All-State athlete that they used to applaud and cheer for. A white woman drove up in her car and told the two white men to stop hitting on her and when they told her to mind her business, she pulled out a hunting rifle and aimed it at them, telling them that she would shoot one of them like a deer in the woods, when they left Sheila alone and the woman taking Sheila to a hospital. When the short, burly white woman with gnarled black hair and a rifle strapped around her shoulder brought Sheila into the hospital, the doctors and some sympathetic nurses waved her away, telling her to take the bleeding and broken black woman to a 'Colored Only' hospital! She put Sheila in a chair in the lobby and drew her rifle, telling the frightened hospital staff "Fuck the **Only** sign in the window!" and to help the black woman, when two officers with guns came upon her and told her to 'Take the injured nigger woman somewhere else, or she could join her,' then left the hospital with a badly hurt Sheila in her truck.

The woman drove ten miles outside the town of Shiloh to her cabin so she could tend to Sheila's wounds, not knowing of any 'Colored' hospitals in the area and wanting to get out of harm's way. The woman sedated a half-conscious Sheila and set her dislocated shoulder and broken finger, then walking around her cabin drinking her homemade 'moonshine' and talking to her dog Spartacus about how cruel and ignorant people are, with the dog barking in agreement. The cabin was remote from the town of Shiloh and having been a nurse for several years, she was well equipped to tend to Sheila's injuries without the interference of racist people in the town of Shiloh. Two days had passed since the incident in the parking lot and Sheila was coming around from her grogginess, asking the strange woman who she was and where they were at? She was vague about answering both questions, only telling Sheila that she was safe and that the two white men that assaulted her should be hung from a tall tree in her backyard, when she noticed police lights in the front of her cabin. She told Sheila that everything would be alright and grabbed her rifle, motioning to her dog to stay put, then went outside to confront the Shiloh County Police.

"Howdy, Mam! Would you be Ms. Lorretta Barrow?"

"Who's asking?"

"Well, mam, me and my partner are looking for a colored woman."

"What for?"

"For assaulting a couple of white people at a store she shouldn't have been at, besides, we got eyewitnesses that seen your truck in the parking lot, Ms. Barrow!"

"Excuse me, but aren't you 'kin' to that Clyde Barrow that got killed for robbing banks?"

"You'll have to excuse my partner, he lacks manners and is new to these parts, but you could answer his question, are you 'kin' to Clyde Barrow?"

"Yes, we were cousins! So, you mean to tell me that one black woman beat-up and assaulted three white people, are you ignorant or just plain stupid!"

"Listen, we know she's here and we're taking her to the police station, now go in and get the nigger woman out here or we'll go in and get her!"

"If you try to take that girl out of my house, I'll do things to the both of you that your mother's never told you about!"

With the tensions rising to a 'Mexican stand-off,' Sheila walked out of the house, battered and bruised, and thanked the woman that cared for her, telling her she didn't want her to get into trouble for something she had to deal with. The police officers were leading her into the police car like a criminal, when one of the officers got a little physical with Sheila, causing the woman to pump her shotgun and the officers being more careful while putting her in the car. A day later when she went to court with her sister Lydia in attendance, Sheila's lawyer told the court of her athletic accomplishments and going to college, even after the death of her mother from cancer, and it was an unfortunate incident that would never happen again. The lawyer for the town of Shiloh told the all-white jury, "Regardless of Ms. Sheila Thompson's accomplishments, we cannot and will not tolerate 'Negroes' going around assaulting 'God fearing' white people, because if they do, there are consequences and repercussions for those actions!" The jury came back with a guilty verdict and went to lunch like they breathe air, feeling a sense of pride for defending the rights of the people of Shiloh against a black menace, then putting away in their conscience's what would become of the promising young black woman, regardless of her telling the court about the sexual taunts and gropings from the two white police officers that arrested her. The judge sentenced Sheila to 18 months at The Women's Correctional Facility on the edge of the town of Shiloh, thus ending her scholarships from 'dirt patch university for girl's' and becoming a hardened, but still caring person of 20 years old in 1947. Once in a while the women were allowed to play records on Friday nights, and Billie Holiday was a favorite among the women at the correctional facility in Shiloh. It didn't take Sheila Thompson long to establish herself at the facility by being respectful to those around her, but knowing that the well-built, good natured girl could handle herself in a fight, having already beaten up one of the toughest women in the facility known as 'Krazy Karen' and was put in solitary confinement for three months for the offense. Most of the correctional officers, and some of the women, began calling her 'Ms. Sheila' soon after her release from solitary confinement, and began to treat her as if she would be there longer than she was sentenced.

Part V
Big Joe goes home.

The boys were busy with their semi-professional obligations to Mr. Walcott and when there was down time, Mr. Walcott kept them busy by having them run 'numbers' for him and other errands, but nothing to jeopardize their promising futures. Mr. Lassiter was the one that kept an eye on the boys and when they got out of line, he reprimanded them and told them that they were no longer 'wide eyed hayseeds' but young men of twenty-four and would be dealing with 'grown-up shit' from now on! Joe Payton was one for being homesick and would often tell James that he wanted to go home, with James reassuring him that they would get some time off and see Sheila and Dahlia and take them to the movies and dances again, but first they had to get things right with Mr. Walcott because of the money Big Joe owed him. The wandering eyes of James Rollins spotted a pretty young 'redbone' girl named Kim that lived with her aunt on the outskirts of Calumet, meeting up with her for 'clandestine interludes' and leaving Big Joe alone to 'fend' for himself on his own wits. When James did set his friend up with a girl, Big Joe would get uncomfortable and start stuttering about how he wanted to go home and marry Sheila Thompson, then leave the room they shared to get some fresh air, sometimes leaving the girl alone in the room for hours.

It was a summer morning in Calumet and the Lincoln Cafe was bustling with people coming and going, and one of those people going was Big Joe Payton, who got fed up with stuttering for permission to go home and see Sheila and his family. He had tried to reach Sheila by calling her on the payphone in the cafe lobby, but got no answer from her father Xavier Thompson's house and wasn't aware that she went to spend time with her sister Lydia in the town of Shiloh. He attempted to write her letters but because of his illiteracy he gave up and threw the half written letters in the trash, thinking he could express his feelings to her better if he were there with her. Mr. Demitrius Lassitter walked into the cafe just as Big Joe was about to leave after finishing his breakfast, when he sat down at Joe's table and asked him where he was going, noticing a suitcase under the table next to his leg? Big Joe looked around the cafe as if he was oblivious to Mr. Lassitter's question, when he nervously stuttered that he was going home to see his 'kin' and his girlfriend Sheila Thompson and that no one was going to stop him from going, when Mr. Lassitter told him he should read a letter that he just got from her before hastily leaving town! Upon hearing that a letter from Sheila had arrived in his room, the large man-child grabbed his worn leather suitcase and hurriedly left the cafe to flag down a cab as if he were late for a flight at the airport, and hoping that when he got to his room he could find someone to help him read the letter?

When he got to the three floored house that was shared by other tenants, Joe paid the cab driver and took two steps at a time to get to the third floor of the room he shared with James, and when he got in after fumbling with his keys he saw a note from James that simply read 'w/k' (with Kim), then the letter from Sheila and walked down the end of the hall to ask the old woman that lived there to read the letter for him. Even with the anxiety rushing through his large body, he gently knocked on the old woman's door while trying to read the strange address on the letter and when she answered his knocks, Big Joe just handed her the letter without stuttering a word as the old woman put her glasses on to read him the letter. He asked her to read the letter from Shiloh to him three times before taking the letter and thanking her, then retreating to his room and locking the door so he could be alone and sob uncontrollably about what happened to Sheila, now more determined than ever to go home. When James came into the apartment after spending time with Kim that evening, he saw a distraught Big Joe crying and drinking liquor on the edge of his bed, then handed him the letter from Shiloh. The letter read of Sheila's racist incident in the town of Shiloh and how she was beaten by two white men, then cared for by a strange woman named Lorretta and the police coming to arrest her at the strange woman's cabin. The letter also went on to tell of how she was 'sexually assaulted' by the two white police officers in the car, but sent to the Women's Correctional Facility in the town of Shiloh for 18 months for slapping a white woman. After reading the letter, James tried to reassure his friend that all would be alright after they settled things with Mr. Walcott and Mr. Lassitter, then they could go to Sometime and straighten things out, when Big Joe Payton lashed out, "F,F, Fuck Mista Walcotts and M,M, Mista Lassitas, I'mz going 'homz' to see my kin and Sheila, and 'gitz' those 'Sonzabitchz' that did this to her!"

It is a hard thing to do to keep a large man calm when he is dealing with pain and duress, but even harder when that large man is your friend and can eclipse the sun with his shadow. The sun was not eclipsed by Big Joe's anger and hurry to leave the town of Calumet when James gave him a big 'whollup' upside his head, knocking Big Joe out until the dusk of the evening settled on the dingy curtains of their room. The coming of the sun had Big Joe waking up on his bed next to the window, shielding his eyes from the sun as they penetrated the stained curtain and looking to see what stains looked like figures or faces. He got up and stretched out his large body and rubbed his head and felt a 'knot' where James had punched him, then saw a note on the table for two that read 'w2cK (when to see Kim)' and began packing again to go home. While he was getting ready to leave and probably never come back to the town of Calumet again, Demitrius Lassitter knocked on his door and let himself in and asked him where he was going in such a hurry? He told him that he was going to the bus depot and catching the next bus to the town of Sometime, because his girlfriend Sheila was in trouble and he was homesick and he didn't care much for the people in town. Mr. Lassitter offered him a ride to the bus depot and told him that James had paid his debt with Mr. Walcott, when Big Joe thanked him for his hospitality and grabbed his suitcase as he was anxious to catch the bus home but stopped briefly, writing a short note for James that read 'gon hom' then left with Mr. Lassitter.

They got into Mr. Lassitter's long black car and drove towards the bus depot about a mile outside of Calumet, with Big Joe already being a nuisance to Mr. Lassitter with his constant stuttering about how much he loved Sheila Thompson and how he was going to marry her when she got out of jail. After a half hour of driving to the bus depot, Demitrius Lassitter had enough of Big Joe's stuttering soliloquies about his love for Sheila Thompson and pulled over to a roadside diner, telling Big Joe he should 'fuel up' for his long bus ride. They went into the Cagney Diner and ordered some sandwiches and coffee and as it began to rain, Mr. Lassitter looked around the diner as if he expected to see some people he knew, and when he did he told Big Joe that he had to go to the car and roll up the windows so the seats wouldn't get wet. He sat at the counter eating his sandwich and sipping his coffee, periodically looking up at the clock behind the counter so he wouldn't miss the 2:30 pm bus to Sometime, when he looked out the large window of the diner and saw that Mr. Lassitter got into his car and drove away in the rain and before he could stutter a word, four large black men approached him at the counter and asked to speak with him outside.

A gentle summer breeze blew through the house of Mrs. Mary Payton as she was doing her morning chores, when she was interrupted by a loud noise on her front porch as if something heavy had been dropped on it, causing some of her dishes in the cabinet to rattle. She nervously went to the front door and when she opened it, she saw a large burlap sack with a note that read 'gon hom' and when she got a knife out of the kitchen and cut the sack open, she saw the body of her son Joe Payton. Sheila Thompson received the news about Joe's death from his mother during the phone call she was allowed every afternoon, then began screaming and crying hysterically while smashing the phone that the other women at the facility used, causing the correctional officers to subdue her and put her in solitary confinement, again!

With the death of Big Joe and the incarceration of Sheila, James and Dahlia felt their inner circle disintegrating and started looking at options to get away from what was going on around them, even if it meant going their separate ways.

Chapter VI
The Outskirts of Dahlia

Dahlia LeeAnn Black had always been an independent type of person ever since she was young, with her half Iroquois mother Wanda and her mother's sister Mildred taking her on hunting expositions before she could walk. She learned to be kind to people but to never trust them, remembering what her father Atticus used to tell her when he got angry after dealing with white people and their lying ways. Dahlia adored her father and got a lot of her nature from the tall, outspoken black man who spoke up to white people as a man, causing him problems in many different places even though he was a mix of white and Iriquos Indian. For most of his life, Atticus Wendell Black was a trained surveyor and knew his way around the 'anas' better than most people born there, hiring out his services to take people up into the mountains so they could build and kill things, regardless of who got hurt or killed in the process.

Their brief and short union lasted from the high mountains of Indiana to a modest place in the town of Sometime, where Atticus and Wanda settled down and had two children, a boy named Sampson and Dahlia. Wanda Black was a fair skinned woman that would sometimes be mistaken for a white woman, until people got to know her and realized she was no white woman! When he lived in the Canadian territories he was treated and judged by his deeds and moral character, which were upright but dangerous because of his firm belief in killing a person before they killed him. Atticus W. Black was taught these lessons from his mother Alma and grandmother Edna, along with his seventeen brothers and sisters from the book of Psalms in the bible, and other passages about revenge and forgiveness.

The judgment of a man was different a couple hundred miles away, as it was based on skin color and heritage more than anything, and moral character meant very little except for complete capitulation to a racist system. Instead of accepting the brutal system of out dated 'Jim Crow' laws, Atticus and Wanda had their own variety store that sold goods and services that most people needed, and with Atticus having his surveying business and the help of Wanda's sister Mildred, they lived modestly in the town of Sometime. The leaves and wheatfields began to swirl around the midwest as people began to prepare for a harsh winter, according to the Farmers Almanac that had been right for years but ignored, when the Ithaca Lumber and Mining Company contacted Atticus about surveying some land up north in Toronto, Canada. He agreed with the company and thought it would be important for his son Sampson to see some of the country that he came from, besides, the family needed the money and Wanda and her sister Mildred would look after little Dahlia, at least until they returned before the bad weather set in. After a week of preparation and saying good-bye to each other, Atticus and his seven year old son Sampson got into his brown truck and headed for Canada, taking a more dangerous but quicker route known as Crimes Pass.

Dahlia was six years old when her father and brother left for Canada and the rambunctious kid was kept busy, by going to school and helping her mother and aunt Mildred in the store, and sometimes playing with a girl she met named Sheila. Within a week's time and the foretelling of the Farmers Almanac, the weather changed like it did in the bible and tornadoes swept across the midwest, along with rain and snowstorms wiping out almost everything in its path! It was days before people recovered from the storms and were able to get word to one another throughout the 'anas,' trying to find out by word of mouth who survived the storms and who didn't? Wanda Black and her sister Mildred and Dahlia survived the storms and were cleaning up the store days later, when a young man came in and handed Wanda an express letter from The Ithaca Lumber and Mining Company that was written **Open Immediately,** which Wanda did with calm anxiety? She walked off to the corner of the store for some privacy and braced herself for what the letter had in store, and upon opening the letter it read that her husband Atticus Wendell Black and her son Sampson Wendell Black were both killed, when the truck her husband was driving lost control on Crimes Pass during the storm and crashed into the mountainous terrain below. With the deepest sincerity that the Ithaca Lumber and Mining Company could fake in a letter for the loss of Atticus and her son, there was a check for the amount of $2,550.00 dollars for the work Atticus 'would' have done for the company, with Wanda thinking that the company wanted more from her husband than just surveying some land up north for that kind of money? Having read the bad news in the telegram and thinking how she didn't tip the delivery boy, Wanda talked to her sister about the loss and they began going into a 'mourning for death' state of mind, which is a sense of mourning in the Iroquois tradition of no outsiders! These would be the things that Dahlia remembered from her mother and aunt Mildred throughout her life as she grew to love people, but never to trust them because of what her father Atticus had told her before he died.

Part I
A different kind of friend.

Dahlia Black grew up remembering the loss of her father and older brother and carried that hurt with her wherever she went, even within her 'inner circle' years later when they would ask her why she seemed so distant, and wanting to go to Italy and Egypt so badly before she died? When it came time for Dahlia's final year of school she begrudgingly returned to Sonoma Valley College, not wanting to return to the 'patch of dirt for girls' university after the incarceration of her best friend Sheila Thompson and the killing of Big Joe Payton. She went through school as if in a trance like her mother and aunt had shown her, and the other students were just blurs passing her by when a girl approached her and said she was sorry to hear about what happened to Sheila, and if she wanted to hang-out sometime just to let her know. Dahlia walked around for the remainder of the day somewhat dumbfounded, not really knowing how to talk to another student directly without Sheila being there, and decided to confront the girl the next time she saw her.

It wasn't long before Dahlia saw the tall, caramel colored girl with long black hair and approached her, asking her who she was and how she knew Sheila? The impressive looking girl told her that her name was April Carrington and that she was from Juaniqua County, way up north and had just transferred to Sonoma Valley College, and that she didn't know Sheila that well except for saying 'hello' in passing. They slowly began talking about school and what happened to Sheila, and Dahlia slowly began to let her guard down with the strange girl from up north, who surprisingly told Dahlia that her mother was Chinese-American and her father was a black man with Indian blood. When his schedule allowed it and his 'errands' for his new boss Mr. Hagler had been taken care of, James Rollins would go and see Dahlia and spend time with her, but their other interests were beginning to show in their relationship. James would talk about baseball and making money with Mr. Hagler, while Dahlia would talk about the Zora Neale Hurston books she was reading, and how nice it would be to travel to other parts of the world. They talked about their dreams and aspirations that they wanted in life, but were beginning to realize that those dreams and aspirations didn't include each other.

The dreariness and monotony of 'patch of dirt university for girls' was lifted for Dahlia with her new found friendship with April Carrington, who went to Dahlia's athletic events and listened to her well into the night about Zora Neale Hurston and anthropology, and how much she missed her father Atticus and brother Sampson. It wasn't long before Dahlia asked April to move in with her in the apartment she used to share with Sheila, and once April accepted her offer and moved in, Dahlia felt that this was a different kind of friendship?

Part II
The solitude of Juaniqua County.

The brutal storms that plagued the 'anas' during post war America gave way to the hot, dry summers and while many families were going to the Grand Canyon on summer vacations, other families were swinging pickaxes and hoes into barren grounds just to make a living. It was the last year of school for Dahlia and she was looking forward to her degree in anthropology, inspired by the life of her favorite writer Zora Neale Hurston and planned on spending the summer with her mother and aunt up north to do some 'biblical' hunting in the woods, when April invited her to go up north to Juaniqua County for the summer? Dahlia was surprised at her asking that, considering they shared an apartment away from school where their 'relationship' was private and as Dahlia was pondering her question, April began telling her how nice Juaniqua County is with streams that flow with fish and the deer and Elk roam around as if they owned the land. She told Dahlia that the sun rose above the trees and mountains as if it were the only place on earth, and the solitude they could share being away from the skeptical, lying people that surrounded them. Dahlia agreed to go with April up north to the tranquility and solitude of Juaniqua County, having for the first time in quite a while a 'loving' relationship with someone outside of her father and brother, her mother and aunt Mildred, James, Sheila and Big Joe, and a stray cat named Socrates.

Soon after the mesmerizing description of Juaniqua County, Dahlia and April were packed up and driving up north in Dahlia's brown truck to a place she never heard of or seen, and her mother and father knew almost every inch of the northern country and remembering not to take Crimes Pass to get there. Once they got out of Sometime and headed for the Canadian border, April took over driving into the remote parts of the 'anas' as Dahlia read **How it feels to be Colored Me** and asked April questions about 'who' she was? April told her that she had three older brothers but the youngest one, December Carrington, was killed in World War II but her two other brother's, October and November Carrington lived around Juaniqua County. Dahlia stopped reading her book and asked April if everyone in her family was named after a month in the year, when she told her that her mother's name was May and her father was called 'Mr. January.'

Their drive to Juaniqua County required an overnight stay in the woods with sleeping bags and kerosene lamps, as they looked at the touchable stars and Dahlia reading parts of her Zora Neale Hurston book to April. She began counting the stars in the sky and pointed out the 'Big and Little Dipper,' when she told Dahlia that she never had a best friend growing up and could never replace Sheila, but wanted to try because she was in love with her! Dahlia stopped reading her book and looked at April intently, as if April had violated something personal with her and told April to never cross her and to keep their relationship between them private, or she would never have anything to do with her again, then went back to reading her book before they fell asleep in a large sleeping bag together.

When they reached Juaniqua County and got to April's parents' home her mother and father were glad to see her, as her mother would cry every time she was around her children after the loss of her son December, but welcomed her daughter and her new friend to their home while Mr. January Carrington watched from the living-room of the house. After the gracious greeting from her mother May Carrington and the somewhat reserved reception from her father, April was given the keys to the large 'tree house' in the back of the family property, which had miraculously survived the storms and was reinforced on Mr. Carrington's instructions. After talking with her mother and having a loving, but distant, good-bye with her father, April left and drove Dahlia a short distance to a secluded place in the woods on the property and pulled up to a large Oak tree, then showed her the 'tree house' they would be staying in and Dahlia was stunned! There was a spiral staircase wrapped around a large Oak tree that led to an apartment sized 'tree house,' with electricity and a radio playing country songs when they got in, and as they settled into their summer residence, Dahlia began to feel the solitude of Juaniquea County that April had described to her back in Sometime.

Part III
When April ends.

The time in Juaniqua County was just as April had said it would be, with the fish in the streams and the four-legged creatures roaming the countryside like they owned it and Dahlia and April fishing and hunting but never killing anything, and sharing 'personal' moments together in their solitude. They were both in love with each other but in different ways, with April thinking that she could travel with Dahlia to Egypt and Italy as an assistant with her anthropology expeditions, and Dahlia beginning to feel the need to go back to the town of Sometime with her mother and aunt Mildred, and the thoughts of strangely reuniting with James? Their summer of solitude was coming to an end, with April telling Dahlia that they should live together in her treehouse apartment, while Dahlia remained silent during April's questions about them living together? A warm summer evening after spending the day together had a jittery Dahlia pacing the treehouse, as April Carrington got comfortable with a false sense of being with Dahlia for the rest of her live and as she slumbered under the quiet singing of birds in the tree, Dahlia wrote her a note.

 It was said by April to Dahlia that the sun rising in Juaniqua County was as if it were the only place on earth, and when Dahlia rose with it she quietly made her way down the spiral staircase that wrapped around the large Oak tree, trying not to disturb April as she quietly got into her truck and headed for Some time. April woke up a little after the birds stopped singing and rubbed her eyes in the sunshine from the window and stretched her taught body, when she saw a note from Dahlia on the table they shared and read it. The note from Dahlia read that she was going back to Sometime and enjoyed the solitude of the treehouse and the 'Eden' of Juaniqua County, but had to return home because of her strong bond with her mother after the death of Atticus and her brother

Sampson! There was a small p.s. in the note that told how much Dahlia loved her and after reading that part, April stayed in the treehouse alone for days on end, which caused her parents to become concerned about her well-being? She would occasionally come out of her treehouse to drive the long pathway to the house to get some food, occasionally telling her mother during their brief conversations that she was fine with Dahlia leaving, and that she wouldn't be returning to school in the fall.

After three days of not seeing or speaking with her daughter, May Carrington got in her car and drove the short distance to her daughter's treehouse, and when she got there she climbed the spiral staircase and pushed April's half open door. When the door opened, May began to cry as she always did when she saw her children but this time for a different reason, as she saw the once beautiful, caramel colored complexion of her daughter now a pale shade of blue lying in bed with an empty bottle of sleeping pills on the floor, and a note on her nightstand table that read, 'I loved you too, Dahlia'!

Part IV
It's in my nature.

When Dahlia returned home to the town of Sometime not much had changed during her summer away, as her mother and aunt Mildred maintained the now Atticus Merchant Company which supplied local merchants and townsfolk with goods and traveling necessities when they traveled up north to hunt for the winter, or needing surveying through the treacherous terrain. It was now the year of 1950 and another black man 'not' named Louis was the heavyweight champion of the world, while the President of the United States got the country involved in a secret little war in Korea that finally got James Rollins away from the gangsters in the town of Calumet in Illinois. He joined the Army after finding out that the 'boss' of the Calumet Syndicate, Mr. Hagler wanted to have him killed for killing two men that were involved in the beating death of his friend Joe Payton. The President desegregated the military and some white men had a hard time dealing with a black man as an equal, even though they were in a foreign country and death by the enemy had no color. He was sent to Korea and served in the Infantry Division where the battles were fierce and bloody, with most American soldiers getting confused about 'who' they were supposed to kill because all the Korean soldiers, North or South, looked the same? After some extreme fighting in a small South Korean province, James was paired with a white soldier named Tyrus Van Meter to go on a scouting mission about enemy advancement, when Tyrus told his commanding officer, "I'm not going on any mission with a nigger, he'll probably try to kill me!" The commanding officer could care less about Tyrus' racist views and sent them on the scouting mission anyway, with James telling Tyrus as they were preparing to leave that 'One day the chickens will come home to roost for him' and Tyrus ignoring what James was saying to him.

They were both hurt on the mission that killed many soldiers from both sides and shipped back to the states, with James nervous about going back to Sometime and Tyrus not really knowing where he wanted to go? Another winter was fast approaching the midwest and as James was recovering from his injuries at his parents' home, Dahlia had received a letter from May Carrington about April's death by suicide and began an Iriquous way of mourning, which included isolation and emotional distance from other people. There was a strange look in her eyes when she packed a few belongings to go on a retreat up in the mountains, with her mother Wanda and aunt Mildred blessing her as she left for her retreat, knowing that what she was doing was in her nature. When James had recovered enough from his injuries he went to the Atticus Merchant Company to see Dahlia, and when he couldn't find her he spoke with Wanda Black, who told him that Dahlia was on a 'spiritual retreat' up in the mountains to mourn the loss of a friend. When James left the store he had a pretty good idea of where to find Dahlia up in the mountains and went home, preparing to take a trip into the mountains and find Dahlia so he could ask her to marry him. He drove through the Solace Mountains and came upon a remote campsite where he saw Dahlia but could hardly recognize her, as she had been up in the mountains for days and looked like a 'beautiful wild animal' and James was cautious to approach her.

When James got out of his truck and approached her, Dahlia looked at him as if she wanted to kill him with the hunting knife in her hand, then loosened her grip on the knife when she realized it was James and gave him a slight smile.

"Dahlia, what on God's earth are you doing up here by yourself, way up in the Solace Mountains?"

"I'm mourning the loss of a close friend and I didn't realize how close, until I got a letter in the mail a few days ago."

"Was the letter about Sheila, how's she doing?"

"Time, that's what she's doing James, and the letter wasn't from Sheila!"

"Listen Dahlia, I've seen some 'fucked up shit' when I was in Calumet and the war over in Koerea, but this 'mourning' thing your doing is some weird shit and who would send you a letter to make you do this?"

"You don't know the person, I met her at school after Sheila went to jail and you were in Calumet with Big Joe and he got killed, so we just became close."

"Why did you have to come all the way up into the mountains to mourn, did she die or something?"

"It's an Iroquois way of mourning, it's in my nature."

"Will your 'nature' allow me to take you back to civilization and get you cleaned up, because I'm not going to marry you looking like that, shit, I just got back from Korea!"

The long, winding roads led Dahlia back to 'civilization' and she washed the mourning of the Solace Mountains off her body and mind, then married James and became Dahlia Black-Rollins with thoughts of being a good wife and mother, but still with aspirations of going to Italy and Egypt.

Chapter VII
The World Amplified

Time is the healer of all wounds and many of them were healed throughout the town of Sometime, as Becky recovered from her injuries at 'the park' and developed a fierce competitive spirit, which made her the best girls' basketball player in the country in 1969 at the age of seventeen, but the girls from Sonoma High School never heard from Wendy Monroe again. There was an independent, rebellious spirit with black people in the country, as the ways of 'Jim Crow' were slowly giving way to desegregation and the sustained efforts of the Civil Rights movement. With a decade of the country witnessing the killing or assassinations of any leader worth substance and an escalating war in a small place called Vietnam, many young people of both races protested against the countries 'underhanded' tactics and were met with the same indifference as if they were the enemy!

During the times of political unrest and a hated Muslim having his title taken from him because of a war, Becky involved herself with young activists wanting to make change for black people in the country but only going so far with it, as she didn't want to jeopardize her scholarships to colleges. The society that Becky was now growing up in was different from her parents James and Dahlia, and her grandmother Wanda and great aunt Mildred were completely clueless about the changing times and the world becoming amplified. It was no longer the times of gray steel monsters from space and the white man was always right, but a generation of psychedelic colors and music that liberated the country into color. The country's business was now exposed by 'The most trusted man in America' on television every night and with Jimi Hendrix amplified around the world, a group of black people in California decided to exercise their 2nd Amendment Rights and started carrying guns and weapons.

She was a young girl in her times, but was not of her times, as Becky didn't drink alcohol nor smoked tobacco but enjoyed the smell of it from her grandmother and great aunt's corn pipes, but would 'tighten up' when her grandmother Wanda would share stories with her sister about how she used to cut negroes' down from trees after they'd been hung and gave them proper burials. Both of her parents were surprised at her growth, or as her aunt Mildred would say 'sprouting like a weed' and was nearly six-feet, four inches tall, when she went against her mother's wishes and decided to go to 'patch of dirt university for girls' at Sonoma Valley College. The store's name was now the Atticus/Sampson Mercantile and Exchange Company, which provided Dahlia a way to go on expeditions with a group of people into the Solace Mountains and James working a Civil Servant job as an engineer because he blew up a bridge in Korea. Once she arrived at Sonoma Valley College and with the burgeoning of sports media because of a guy named Joe that played for the Jets in New York, the 'patch of dirt university for girls' was highlighted in sports magazines and television snippets of the best girls college basketball player in the country, averaging 32 points, 15 rebounds and 12 assists a game for the undefeated Sonoma Valley College Iroquois Riders, which brought cameras and strange people asking Becky questions about who she was and why she played basketball in a patch of dirt in the 'anas'?

    She remained close with her friends Megan, Jackie and Naomi even though they went to separate schools, but continued to speak with Sara by phone or letter who had moved farther up north with her aunt and was attending an agricultural college, and continued to write letters to Rebeca in the 'girls' jail' in Dire even if it could get her into trouble? There was a quiet buzz with the young people in the country about a music festival in upstate New York and many decided to go, with most thinking that it would be nothing more than a few hundred people and a handful of performers. The three girls that Becky knew from school talked about going to the festival, but only Megan Blake decided to go with some friends she met at her school. When she arrived at the festival called Woodstock it was not the intimate setting that the shy, naive Megan was expecting, but a mass of thousands that resembled the Israelites fleeing Egypt and was swept up in the crowd. The white girl and two other black girls that Megan went with searched for her throughout the day's long festival, even asking a young black guitar player if he had seen their friend? The festival had ended and days turned into weeks as the young people that attended were still trying to clear their ears from the amplified event, as word got to Becky from Jackie and Naomi that another one of their friends had gone missing!

After hearing about the disappearance of her friend Megan, Becky took some time off of school and met with Sara Blackfoot to go on a 'retreat' into the Solace Mountains and mourn the loss of Megan, with the blessing and approval of her mother, grandmother and great-aunt Mildred and her father James telling her not to get lost like her mother did some years back. While they were on Becky's 'retreat' to mourn in the Iroquois tradition but this time with a radio, Sara read a letter that she had recently received from Rebeca about being released from Dire soon, and how she hated the fact that her grandmother Mildred Dean would have custody of her while living on the family farm, and after Sara read the letter and put it into the box of saved letters between them, they talked about how most women in the 'anas' have the names Mildred or Rebeca or Dorothy, and their friend getting out of the 'girls jail' soon and what she'd be like?

Part I
The color of hate.

The world was now in color and everything it did was no longer in black and white, but with pictures of little children in Asia running naked for their lives because of a war that interrupted their playing with other children, and a spaceship that went to the moon with white men aboard and came back to earth for the world to see in magazines and on billboards, alongside with America's favorite television shows with commercials reassuring that the country was fine and in good hands. During her time of incarceration in the Reformatory for Wayward Girls in the town of Dire, Rebeca spent five years without seeing much color in the gray town she spent with other girls, where the sun was afraid to shine and pretty colored flowers were far away. With her continued repentance for killing her father to nuns, priests, psychologists, doctors,' teachers, wardens of the facility, and people that took out the trash, Rebeca Stanwyck Dean Van Meter was released into the custody of her grandmother on a rainy day in 1970. Most of the colors that Rebeca remembered were the colors of the trees on the Aianta cliff and Becky's skin color and Sara's white smile, along with her mother's long brown hair that she brushed obsessively and her red lipstick, and the corruptible smell of alcohol and Brute on her father. Before leaving Dire and being told that she would return someday by the 'experts' that examined and criticized her, Precious Johnson gave her a painting she made of

Shaquon Rutherford looking out of the cell window they shared and the painting showing a sad melancholy in Shaquon's face, which Precious painted shortly after Shaquon Rutherford hung herself in the girl's bathroom. When she came out of the dark, gray institution she was immediately struck and blinded by the light she hadn't seen in five years, when her grandmother Mildred Dean steadied her and led her into her truck, telling her granddaughter that the same thing happened to Saul on his way to Damascus. She got into her grandmothers' black truck and drove off from the only home she had known for five years, looking out the back window of the truck and watching Precious Johnson waving good-bye to her from behind a fence, then thought about Becky and Sara and the looks on their faces when she first started her journey in the back of a police car.

Her grandmother made idle talk about the things going on at the family farm and how she would enjoy being there, and as Rebeca was looking at all the different colors around her as her grandmother drove outside of Dire, she remembered that she had a hatred for just about everything around her except for Becky and Sara. Her grandmother continued to drive into the civilization outside of Dire and mentioned how she had visited her daughter at the 'clinic' in Illinois, when Rebeca remembered how Dorothy would talk to her about the pretty colored trees in Illinois but how she hated people and killed a man in Missouri for not paying her enough attention. Now she was going to live with people that liked her father Tyrus and knew that she killed him, but remembering that her grandmother hated her father and she liked her grandmother's horse named Gunsmoke. They stopped off at a roadside diner and when they entered, the handful of customer's conversations got lower and some men took their hats off as Mildred Dean and her grand-daughter sat at a booth and ordered some food. The people in the diner were talking about the influential woman that just walked in, and who the scruffy looking young girl was that was with her? The food came to the table and Rebeca stared at it for a while, as she was not used to eating such good food, when her grandmother stopped looking at the clouds passing in the sky from the window at the booth, and asked her if she had been Saved by Christ?

"Saved by Christ, yes Grandma Dean! I got saved when I killed my father and survived that desolate institution we just left! My friend Shaquon Rutherford hung herself in the girl's bathroom because nobody gave a shit about her and my mother's in a mental institution surrounded by pretty trees, yes, I'm 'Saved' grandma!"

"I did what I could for your mother ever since she was a child, but she just kept getting into trouble that she couldn't get out of, then she married that lying, two-faced pedophyle, west coast piece of shit daddy of yours! It's not your fault for what you did, because if you didn't kill Tyrus Van Meter, I would have!"

"Grandma, before I killed Tyrus I discussed it with my friends Becky and Sara and they told me because of what he was doing to me, he would eventually kill me or put me in a mental institution like my mother, so we took a vote and I killed him!"

"I try to live a righteous life by the Lord and treat people fairly, but I won't tolerate any bullshit or wickedness from people, those are the ones that get 'smited' by the hand of God! There was a woman around these parts that used to cut down hung negroes and bury them, and I met her and didn't even know it was her because she looked like a white woman?"

"That's a strange thing to happen grandma, a white woman riding around on a horse through the hills and mountains and cutting down dead black people from trees, and then having the decency to bury them? That sounds like a very strange woman, but the Christian thing to do!"

"You have been forgiven for your sin of murder by Christ the Lord, and He, the Christ, knowing that I would have killed that 'sonofabitch' Tyrus myself, will do my best to see that you won't be hurt like you were ever again!"

"I lived in a gray place called Dire for five years for killing my father, and I just started hating everything, everyone, and every letter I got about one of Becky's friends disappearing, or Sara being treated like backwater Indian trash and having to move up north! I sometimes wonder if hate has a color, like when I was little and everything was in black and white, but now it's all in color and louder."

"Rebeca, hate has no color, it's like the clouds that pass in the sky or the rising and setting of the sun, or when the moon is a different color or shape and we're all still confused about why oceans get angry? The only hate that has a color is the color of a person's blood that runs through their body, and I've shot a person or two in my day, even some Ku Klux Klan 'sonofbitches' on our land with your mother!"

"I'll do my best to be a good grand-daughter and get used to all the color around me, and not to hate as much as I do around folks when we get to the farm."

"You'll make a fine grand-daughter, I'll see to that, now finish your meal because it's getting late."

Part II
Gunsmoke by the river.

The Dean family had come a long way from the days of running moonshine and illegal gambling from The Han in Sin City, and were a respected and feared family throughout the 'anas' and farther north and south because of the ruthless ways of Rebeca's grand-father, Mr. Jamison Dean, who had a way of holding on to certain ways from the midwest. It was not an easy transition for Rebeca from the town of Dire to having her own cabin on the family property, and her grandmother spread the word throughout the 'anas' that the young girl staying with her was her dead sister Caroline's daughter from Missouri! The last name Van Meter was removed from her name and she was Rebeca Stanwyck Dean, with a seemingly clean slate as she enrolled at Aurora State University to study psychology and try out for the girls' basketball team. During her time on the semi-isolated farm away from people but close enough to hate them, Rebeca was taught by her grandmother how to ride a horse and drive a stick-shift truck, with daily readings from the bible and distant looks from her grandfather.

Mrs. Mildred Dean rode her favorite horse Gunsmoke down by the river that he liked every morning, then stopped to read the bible by the sounds of the passing river and shot at certain fast moving animals, with the smell of gunsmoke in the air that was carried by the river towards other people nearby. By the time Rebeca arrived on the family farm her grandmother had already had three horses named Gunsmoke during her lifetime, all sired by her first horse named Gunsmoke and named all the male horses she would ride after him. Grandma Dean didn't want Rebeca driving or walking around the vast acres of land and getting lost so she gave her Gunsmoke' s daughter, a pretty brown and white horse named Miss Kitty that Mrs. Dean named after her dead older sister Catherine 'Kitty' Dean. One Sunday morning after church and the Pentecostal preaching of hell and repentance, Rebeca was told by a person working on the property to meet her grandma down by the river for a special occasion and when she got there on her horse Miss Kitty, there was only the sound of the river and Gunsmoke grazing by it, as if he knew they were coming. Without any hesitation or fuss, Mrs. Dean came out from the wooded area and lead Rebeca into the river to baptize her as she had known all her life, and when the currents of the river began to flow stronger Rebeca resisted, but then remembered what her mother had told her about her 'baptism' in the same river some years back, then let her grandma do her 'John the Baptist' impersonation and when she came up from the cold river water all she saw was Gunsmoke by the river looking at her and for his daughter Miss Kitty.

Part III
The girl who killed her father and Eden Winter.

Most of the time since she was released from Dire, Rebeca went to school with her head on a swivel and waiting for someone to point her out and say 'That's the girl who killed her father,' but those shouts weren't heard as she no longer had the Van Meter name to taint her future goals and aspirations. She made the Aurora State University girls basketball team after another player got hurt and averaged 17 points, 5 rebounds and 10 assists a game, thinking how 'soft' the girls she played against were compared to her fights in Dire, but mindful not to lose her temper during games or practices for fear of someone knowing who she really was? Since she had been back in the town of Sometime her letters to Becky were now nonexistent, and she didn't even know if Sara was still alive even though they all shared taking out the trash and their 'sisterly bond' on Aianta cliff.

Her grandmother taught her how to ride her favorite horse Miss Kitty throughout the family farm and beyond, and taught her the righteousness of the bible and how God's word never lies, along with how to shoot a rifle and a gun in case the Ku Klux Klan showed up on her doorstep one day when she got older and how to cuss when it was necessary. Her grandfather Jamison Dean treated her in a 'passing' way, only saying 'hello or how's your mother' and the customary 'nice day today' to her when he saw her, and she felt that her grandfather hated her for killing Tyrus because he liked him and did criminal things for him. It was 1970 and Mr. Jamison Dean still talked about black people like it was the Civil War, even though he was known throughout the 'anas' as a fair and just Pentecostal man. On a day at a family gathering on the Dean property in the town of Fairmont, her Uncle John Dean showed her too much affection away from his wife and three kids by hugging her too closely, reminding Rebeca of her father's aftershave and asked to speak with him privately. They went into a barn and John Dean had other thoughts on his mind with the well-built, troubled young girl, when Rebeca pulled out a shotgun hidden in the barn and told her Uncle John Dean, "If you ever hug me like that again, I'll get to thinking that you love me, like my daddy did, and you know what happens when we show too much love in this family!"

There were no more hugs from Uncle John and during the next couple of years Rebeca did well at Aurora State University, looking forward to getting her degree in sociology, having switched from psychology when her grandmother told her that most people are liars and full of shit, and God deals with the rest of them. She still played on the basketball team and heard about how Becky Black Rollins was the best female basketball player in the country, missing seeing her by only a couple of miles when their basketball teams would crisscross the midwest on buses to play other teams. There were rumors about her and how most of the girls had never seen her when they were growing up, but once the rumors got to grown people they were quickly dispelled by Mrs. Mildred Dean, who would not tolerate any disrespect regarding her dead sister Catherine's name or her 'values,' and the grand-daughter she left behind before she died and was now caring for!

It was a cold day in December when Aurora State University traveled to Kansas to play Wichita Valley State, which had the toughest, most intimidating player in college basketball named Eden Winter. She was all of six-feet, five-inches of backwoods Kansas and was known to chew tobacco on the bench, then spit it on the opposing team's bench when she passed it and saying nasty, personal things about girl's personal business, causing them to cry and lose their composure and games. Surprisingly, there were many people in the stands as black and white people 'almost' sat together in 1974 Kansas and the much anticipated game began, with Eden Winter spitting tobacco on Rebeca's sneakers and telling her she knew who she was and what she did! The game went back and forth on the cold December night in Kansas, as people in the stands shared hot cocoa mixed with liquor to warm themselves up as Eden Winter knocked Rebeca around the basketball court and said things to her like, "I know you're the girl that killed her father! How was the town of Dire? Made any new friends since that 'Injun' girl hung herself?" Rebeca got rattled but remembered not to lose her temper as only a handful of people could hear what Eden Winter was saying, and did not want to jeopardize graduating and losing all she had been through just to be in a cold gymnasium in Kansas. The game ended with Wichita Valley State winning 79 to 75 and Rebeca feeling like she did when she was alone in the basement before she killed her father, alone with no one to protect her as she sat on the bench crying, not realizing that Sonoma Valley College was watching the game to see who they would be playing next in the Midwest tournament. After the game there were a few local newspaper articles about Wichita Valley State's big win over Aurora State University, and questions asked to Eden Winter about the girl that killed her father?

Part IV
Revenge for my friend!

It was one of the first integrated girls' college basketball games to be played on national television, as Wichita Valley State prepared to play against Sonoma Valley College for the Midwest Regional Championship, with both star player's holding grudges against one another. Before the game started, Rebeca wanted to spend time with her mother Dorothy and was allowed to stay at The Heinrich Institute in Illinois overnight, while her mother watched old Barbara Stanwyck movies and asked her mother if she could watch the game when it came on? Rebeca brushed her mother's hair obsessively and talked about how much she hated the girl Eden Winter from Kansas, and how she should have punched her in the mouth when she talked about her killing Tyrus, when her mother began talking about getting baptized in the Redemption River and wanting to kill Tyrus Van Meter herself, when the game came on in color and surprised Dorothy because she never seen colored people on television before?

    A black man that had his Heavyweight Championship taken away from him because of a dirty war in Asia, was now the Heavyweight Champion of the World, again, but this time loved and adored by the same country that would have discarded him into obscurity and bringing back a sense of 'Black Pride' in the country, as Becky faced off against Eden Winter on national television for the rights to play in the Women's NCAA Championship. When the much anticipated game started it was evident on T.V. that the cheerleaders from Sonoma Valley University had dirt on their uniforms, and Becky had tobacco spit on her sneakers from the rough and tumble Eden Winter. As the game progressed on national television, a frustrated Eden Winter was heard yelling things at

Becky about her friend being a 'daddy killer' while pointing her finger and taunting her, telling Becky that the same embarrassment she gave to Rebeca was going to happen to her 'boney black ass'! Not wanting to risk her graduation on national television by losing her temper with Eden Winter, Becky dismantled and destroyed Eden Winter and the Wichita Valley State team by scoring 57 points and grabbing 24 rebounds to go with 12 assists and beating them 97 to 80. A despondent Eden Winter was seen on T.V. spitting tobacco at the Sonoma girls' team and throwing chairs on the court, much to the surprise and delight of Rebeca who was still obsessively brushing her mother's hair, when a T.V. reporter asked Becky how she felt about the big win and going to the championship game? With confetti coming down on the basketball court and girls screaming about their dreams being met, Becky said on national television, "This game was revenge for my friend, the girl that killed her father!" When Rebeca heard Becky's words on national television after winning the game, she jumped up and down with excitement while still brushing her mother's hair, causing Dorothy to take the brush away from her and ask Rebeca 'who' the pretty, tall black girl was on T.V.?

Part V
Beyond Sometime.

The televised game put Becky Rollins Black in the national spotlight for her athletic abilities, tall ebony beauty, and her nationwide sound bite of 'revenge' for her friend. With the bright lights of New York City and playing for the Women's College Championship in Madison Square Garden, Sonoma Valley College beat Western Kentucky 87 to 86 with Becky scoring 63 points and grabbing 17 rebounds along with 13 assists and 7 blocked shots. She was soon the 'darling' of Madison Avenue and offered endorsement deals with makeup and fashion companies, along with her pictures in black publications such as **Tej** and ***Ynobe*** magazine wearing the latest fashions and endorsing America's favorite products. Since being on national television and seeing the bright lights of NYC, Becky started thinking of life beyond Sometime and traveling around the world like her mother used to talk about when she was younger, to places like Italy and Egypt.

After a whirlwind of activity and publicity Becky was heading home to the town of Sometime on a bus she traveled many times, when she was offered to play professional basketball in Italy for **Team Nazionale di pallacanestro femminile**, the Italian women's basketball team that traveled the world playing international basketball. With few viable women's pro-leagues in the states, Becky signed a 4-year contract to play professional basketball for Italy in the equivalent amount of $150,000 thousand US dollars, which made her a very rich girl at twenty-two years old. When she arrived in Sometime she was met by her mother at the bus depot and as they drove home, Dahlia told her how proud everyone was of her for winning a national championship for Sonoma Valley College, and that the town was preparing to have a parade for the school's win, but mostly for Becky and her great basketball ability that made it all possible. The reception at home was celebrated in a proud but quiet Iroquois way, as they did not want to boast about their accomplishments but wanted people to know what they had done. Her grandmother Wanda and great-aunt Mildred celebrated Becky's success by thanking God in their Iroquois tradition, then having herbal tea mixed with Indian corn whiskey and sharing a 'peace pipe' from the herbs in their garden, which made everyone around them laugh and gave the four dogs on the property the 'munchies.'

The town of Sometime was preparing for a grand parade for Becky and the Sonoma Valley College girls basketball team, when a close friend of Dahlia's wanted to speak with Becky before the ceremonies began. On a warm Saturday afternoon as Becky was talking to people on the phone about future engagements, and Dahlia was talking to her mother and aunt Mildred about James being gone out of town for so long, when Ms. Sheila Thompson knocked on her front door and when Dahlia answered it, her mother took one look at Ms. Sheila and fainted from surprise, as aunt Mildred began relighting the peacepipe from the night before. When she entered from the shade of the door and the sunlight hit her face it was evident that she was still beautiful, but hardened from her years in Shiloh and as Dahlia and Ms. Sheila hugged like they did before all the 'trouble' started, aunt Mildred tried to revive Wanda by fanning her with a small bamboo fan and blowing 'peace pipe' smoke in her face while trying to give her a sip of 'herbal tea.' They sat at the hand-carved, mahogany table that aunt Mildred had made when she was 17 years old at the reservation for 'troubled' kids, having been sent there because of 'reservation wars' and her involvement with at least two killings and not all being of the animal type.

The now almost fifty-year olds talked about growing up in the town of Sometime and going to 'patch of dirt' university when they were younger, with Ms. Sheila mentioning loudly after two or three 'herbal teas' how her dreams were shattered by the racist white people of Sometime and Shiloh, and how she spent thirteen years in the Women's Correctional Facility. With the evils of the midwest being discussed at the table, Becky walked into the living-room and soon felt as if she had walked in on a sacred ritual, with the four women now looking at her with skeptical, angered faces and Ms. Sheila telling her, "Don't trust any of those 'whitey's' having a parade for you, they'll lie and turn on you just like they did everyone sitting at this table!"

She sat at the table and listened to the four women tell their life stories about growing up in the town of Sometime, and as dusk was setting on the warm summer day, Becky felt older and wiser after listening to the four women at the table while they sipped 'herbal tea' and talked about her future. She told the women that she was looking forward to the parade but after listening to them, she would be looking at the people in a more skeptical way and that she thought about living her life beyond Sometime, not wanting to be a 'casualty' like the four women sitting at the table. The evening was coming to an end and Ms. Sheila was invited to stay the night, as she had too much 'herbal tea' and the roads were too dark for driving, when Becky told them that after the parade she was going to Italy to play for the women's professional basketball team for four years and would be traveling around the world, which made Dahlia stop sipping her 'herbal tea' and look at everyone in the room as if she had just won the lottery!

Part VI
A Convent.

The presidency in America was not the only thing unraveling in 1974, as Rebeca S. Dean started getting asked more questions about who she was, and 'if' she was the girl who killed her father after Becky's nationally televised win and statement on T.V.? After returning to the Dean family farm while visiting her mother Dorothy in Illinois, some neighbors and a few local newspapers around the 'anas' took it upon themselves to inquire about the mysterious niece of Mrs. Mildred Dean. When she went into town, strangers would approach her and just flat out ask her if she killed her father, while a small-time newspaper would have a reporter and photographer taking her pictures and trying to get her to say something. Mrs. Dean had become very protective of her grand-daughter since her release from Dire, helping to transform an angry bottle of energy into a well-spoken, kind young woman that respected the word of God, but could shoot a gun with accuracy and fight if she had too! It was a late summer afternoon and Rebeca was with her Grandma Dean on the back porch of the farm in Fairmont, when Grandma Dean heard rustling in the field near them and saw two men creeping towards the property. She continued to listen to Rebeca talk about strangers asking her rude questions about killing Tyrus, when she quietly grabbed her rifle and aimed it at the two men creeping in the field and as a mild summer breeze blew through the backyard, Grandma Dean fired a shot into the field, then another, when one of the men yelled out "Please don't shoot no more, were just reporters and wanted to get a picture of the girl, I think you might have killed my friend!"

Before the police got to the Dean farm about the shooting, Grandma Dean sent Rebeca home so she wouldn't have to answer the police about another shooting in which she was involved in, and after the near fatal shooting of the photographer from a small midwest newspaper, Grandma Dean told the police that she thought it was the Klu Klux Klan sneaking up on her property like they did a time ago. Ever since the game against Wichita Valley State and the things that Eden Winter had said to her, Rebeca was feeling the pressure and stress of being outside the confinements of Dire and with the recent shooting and near killing of a man on her grandmother's property, it brought back memories of her shooting and killing her father Tyrus and it all caused her to have a nervous breakdown! During Rebeca's nervous breakdown her grandmother tended to her as best she could, but was torn as to what to do with Rebeca as she had dealt with a similar situation with her daughter Dorothy, and did not want to send her grand-daughter back to Dire or where her mother was currently staying. It was an early morning ride on her horse Gunsmoke by the Redemption River that she decided, with prayer and reflection, to put Rebeca in a convent where she would be protected from the so-called 'brood of vipers' that were attacking her, and also praying that Rebeca would not follow in her mother's erratic footsteps.

Grandma Dean made arrangements to have Rebeca picked-up in private at the family farm in Fairmont, away from the harsh criticism of her husband Jamison Dean and the other 'vulchers' that were trying to feast on her repentant grand-daughters soul. With reassurances of love and support, like the kind she tried to show her while she was in Dire, the early morning sun was rising above the plains of the midwest when five nuns dressed in white came to the house to get Rebeca. When Rebeca looked out the window of the room her grandmother always kept for her in Fairmont, the uniforms of the five nuns were brighter than the sun that was rising behind them and became blinded again, just like when she left Dire for the first time and remembered **Paul in the Gospel on the road to Damascus,** then left with the five nuns and her Grandma Dean's blessings. She was going to The Mary Magdalene Convent for Women that was 175 miles away in a town called Repentance, and as she watched her grandmother's figure get smaller on the front porch as the tan station wagon drove away, not knowing how long she would be away from society after they put her away in a convent, she wondered to herself as the nuns drove away from the town of Fairmont if Sara Blackfoot was still alive?

Chapter VIII
A Goddess Among the People

The parade in the town of Sometime was a grand spectacle for many to see, with television cameras filming the event and the white people of the town smiling for the cameras, as if they got along with black people all their lives. During the parade Becky would glance over and see the excitement from her mother and the skeptical looks on Ms. Sheila's face, remembering what she told her about 'not trusting any of the white people at the parade,' as many of the white people proclaimed Becky Black Rollins the town's 'favorite daughter' for the television cameras. Once the parade was over and the confetti already being swept off the street, Becky was presented with many offers from influential people throughout the 'anas,' one being from a wealthy owner of car dealerships that wanted to hire Becky as a showroom model for the newest cars on the market, offering to pay her $10,000.00 dollars a year and travel expenses across the country, telling Becky she would be 'A goddess among the people'! She was smart enough to know that the man would only be using her because of her height and beauty and turned him down, along with all the other offers that were made to her, causing some people to claim that she was being ungrateful to the town of Sometime.

It took a few days after the parade for Becky to get her things together for her trip to Italy, and when she would talk to her mother she noticed that Dahlia would say 'we' are going to have a nice time, or 'we' are going to enjoy Italy, forcing Becky to tell her mother that she was going to Italy alone. Dahlia had already been packing some of her belongings and left word for James that she was going to Italy with Becky, even going so far as to learn Italian words for 'hello' and 'good-bye' and packing all of her Zora Neale Hurston books to read while in Italy. With the devastating news that 'we' now became 'I,' Dahlia retreated in isolation as if mourning the death of a loved one with her dreams of going to Italy and Egypt now shattered, and feeling as most people did in Sometime that Becky was being ungrateful to those that helped her along her journey.

Regardless of her mother Dahlia's hurt feelings and the feelings of some people in the town of Sometime, Becky got into a cab early one Sunday morning and headed for the airport to catch a plane to Italy and once she boarded her flight and the plane took off, she looked out the airplane window and saw the town of Sometime getting smaller and wondered if Sara Blackfoot was still alive?

When she arrived at the airport in Italy the first thing she noticed was the art work, with the airport looking more like an art museum than a place where people were scrambling around to catch flights, then she noticed that she was the tallest person there and didn't really know who to look for to pick her up, as all the people moving around looked the same to her. She began looking through her phonebook to find the agent's number that would be representing her in Italy, when she looked up and saw a young girl holding a black cat and a sign that read **Ciao Becky!** The seventeen year old girl's name was Gloria Loren and she was the niece of the Hollywood actress Sophia Loren, and her cat's name was Barabbas and she was sent by Becky's agent to be her liaison while she was in Italy. The well-dressed but seemingly free spirited young lady stood on a chair, so she wouldn't hurt her neck looking up while talking to Becky, and told her that a taxi cab was waiting for them to take her to the apartment she would be staying at. On the drive to her new place and surroundings through the streets of Italy, Becky thought of how Italy looked so ancient and fragile and how she would fit in, when Gloria told her how she got her cat Barabbas out of an 'animal prison' because he was accused of stealing some rich Italian lady's jewelry, and because she couldn't find her jewelry she blamed the cat and had him sentenced to death!

"Your cat was in a 'animal prison' for stealing?"

"Si, in a prison! Do you know anything about prison, Ms. Becky?"

"Have you ever been to Dire?"

"No, I've never been and just the name sounds like a bad place? Many people here in Italy saw your game on T.V. and thought you were better than most of the players we have on our team. I was surprised to hear that you signed a contract to play over here in Italy!"

"I was surprised too, but I had to get out of Sometime before it killed me one way or another, just like it did Ms. Sheila and my friend Rebeca."

"I hope you don't mind, but me and Barabbas will be your guests in your apartment, per instructions of your agent Victoria Rossi who happens to be my aunt on my mother's side, and me and Barabbas will take the backroom and you can have the large room, considering that you're taller than me."

"I guess I'm stuck with you and Barabbas, besides, I'm going to need someone to help me around this ancient city!"

"Ms. Becky, are you familiar with ancient goddesses?"

"Only Artemisia of Caria, my mother Dahlia is into all that stuff, why?"

"Because Ms. Becky, when you play for the Italian Women's Team and with the help of me and Barabbas, you're going to be a goddess among the people!"

Part I
Zora Neale Hurston meets King Tut.

It was a tough adjustment for Becky when she first got to Italy as she didn't understand her coach's language and made mistakes on the basketball court, causing some to wonder why the team signed this black girl from the midwest for so much Italian lire to play basketball? Besides not understanding the language and the customs of the people around her, she didn't understand Italian food and thought that ketchup was tomato sauce and wine was served at diner only to get drunk! She dressed like a midwestern hillbilly and told Gloria that the men in Italy dressed like 'soft men,' meaning 'homosexual' men and was confused as to 'why' she couldn't carry a gun in public? After a brutal year of retransformation with the help of Gloria and her cat Barabbas, Becky was becoming a refined young woman in style and culture and even started playing better for Team Italia, leading the European Women's League in scoring with 32 points a game while also averaging 7 assists and 15 rebounds.

A year had passed and Becky was getting more accustomed to the ancient buildings that surrounded her loft apartment on Pompeii Avenue, occasionally taking trips with Gloria and her cat to ancient ruins and historical places throughout Italy, which hurt Dahlia even more when she got postcards from Italy showing the places Becky had visited. There was a brief affair with a young man from Argentina that played soccer on the National Team, then a 'relationship' with a handsome young Italian businessman with Mafia connections, with all of her relationships ending because of mistrust and at the insistence of Gloria Loren and her cat Barabbas. With her height, beauty, and God given athletic ability Becky was able to reach new heights in her life, and with a black woman named Ross getting worldwide attention for playing a hard struggling girl that made it 'big' in the fashion industry, the Black magazines from America like **Tej** and ***Ynobe*** descended on Italy. Being the niece of a famous worldwide actress gave Gloria and her cat access to many places around the world, and with Gloria knowing how to speak five different languages from many parts of the world they traveled with Becky to Spain, Russia, Argentina, Sweden, The Netherlands, Africa, France, and an anonymous tournament game in Wichita, Kansas.

It had been over a year since Becky left the town of Sometime and some hurt feelings were now being amended, as she appeared as an extra in a Sophia Loren movie playing a 'goddess among the people' on a small island in the Mediterranean Sea, and in the movie she mentioned how she came from a small town called Sometime! The town of Sometime and the people that live around the 'anas' can be a 'fickle' bunch, like when lynching negros' was commonplace until a 'white' woman rode through the forests and mountains and cut them down from trees and gave them a 'Christian' burial. They thought it was a 'divine' thing for a person to do after they had committed the sin of murder by lynching a person because of their skin color, but when the people of the 'anas' found out it wasn't a 'white' woman cutting down lynched negros' but a half-breed Iriquois woman named Wanda Parker Black and her sister Mildred, some folks wanted to find them and hang them for interfering with the 'Jim Crow' laws of their lands. The marriage between Dahlia and James was strained at best as James occupied his manly urgings outside of Sometime, and Dahlia just going through the motions of everyday life at the store with her mother and aunt Mildred, when a messenger from the post office came to the store with an urgent letter for her. When Dahlia got the letter she immediately looked at her mother and aunt Mildred, who were preparing their Iriquois death ritual because they only knew bad news to be delivered to them, and when she opened the letter it was from Becky that simply read, *C U in Italy, love Becky* with two open ended round trip tickets to Italy! After she held the tickets in her hand and began to realize that her dreams hadn't died, Wanda Parker Black fainted with relief and joy as her sister Mildred relit the peace pipe from the night before and began fanning her sister with a large bamboo leaf to revive her, again! There was also a small letter for Mrs. Wanda Parker Black and her sister Mildred from Ling Kwan, wanting to meet with the both of them in a remote place near the Canadian border?

With excitement and finally getting to go to Italy, Dahlia re-packed her belongings and dusted off all the books she had from Zora Neale Hurston which included ***Dust tracks on a road, Mules and Men, Spunk, Sweat, Their eyes were watching God, How it feels to be Colored me,*** and ***You don't know us Negroes,*** then made reservations to have a cab take her to the airport in the morning and celebrated with her troubled looking mother and aunt during the night. The morning came and Dahlia left another note for James' reading *'Gone to Italy to see Becky, be back?'* then hugged her mother and aunt as the cab arrived to take her to the airport and after the cab left, Wanda Parker Black and her sister Mildred prepared to leave for a remote place near the Canadian border to answer the letter they got from Ling Kwan.

After changing over to a few different airplanes, Dahlia finally arrived in Italy and wandered around the airport looking at all the statues and artwork, when she noticed a free-spirited girl holding a black cat and a sign that read **Ciao Miss Dahlia** and walked over to Gloria and Barabbas. Once she met them, Gloria told Dahlia that Becky was in France for a play-off game against the French Women's Professional Team and that she would be staying in a hotel for a few days, when Dahlia immediately asked her when she could visit the site where King Tutankhamun is buried? Gloria introduced herself and Barabbas to Dahlia and told her that she would be her guide and liaison while in Italy, just as she is for her daughter Becky, and that King Tut was buried in Egypt in a town called Giza which was 2,356 kilometers across the Mediterranean Sea! Before they got into a cab outside the airport an Italian policeman had Barabbas in custody, accused of trying to steal something from a woman's purse and attacking her when the woman tried to take back her belongings, which left Gloria and Dahlia in the airport for another hour until the charges against Barabbas were dropped and he was finally released into Gloria's custody.

They went to the Hotel D'Nero not far from where Becky lived and once Dahlia started unpacking her things, her Zora Neale Hurston books fell out and scattered on the floor, causing Gloria to gasp with excitement and Barabbas to smell every book that fell on the floor. When Gloria went to pick the books up off the floor Dahlia slapped her hands away, causing Barabbas to hiss and hunch up his back as if to attack Dahlia, when Gloria said something sharply in Italian to make Barabbas retreat into a corner, then told Dahlia how Zora Neale Hurston was her favorite writer and how her aunt Sophia loved her books and asked her if she could have one? Dahlia looked over at Barabbas in the corner and with the look on the cat's face, Dahlia gave Gloria the book **Spunk** with the assurances that she would be her guide to Egypt to King Tut's burial site, which Gloria agreed to do, just so long as she could bring her cat? Before they left for Egypt, Gloria got rid of Dahlia's 'hunting to kill' clothing from the 'anas' and styled her in attire from The Black Renaissance Era along with French beret hats, which Dahlia liked a lot and were compliments from Gloria's aunt Sophia.

When they arrived in the ancient town of Giza the rain had finally stopped after three days and a rainbow suddenly appeared, which caused Barabbas to get 'fidgety' and wander off to ancient ruins while Gloria showed Dahlia the places where King Tut lived when he was a boy. After some sightseeing and finally realizing a dream of hers, Dahlia sat on a bench and began reading one of her books when Gloria took a picture of her and said she would send it to Becky in France with the writing, *Zora Neale Hurston meets King Tut!*

Part II
Sometime in the way.

The country was celebrating its Bi-centennial as a nation in the world and as the country celebrated everything red, white, and blue, the sixty-six year old Wanda Parker Black along with her sixty-seven year old sister Mildred got into Wanda's beat-up pick-up truck and headed for the remote town of Solace, to resolve a long standing debt and quarrel with the now seventy-two year old Ling Kwan. It started thirty years back when certain parts of the country would be celebrating the nations birth by lynching negros, when a band of Ku Klux Klan members wanted to find Wanda and her sister and hang them for interfering with their ways of life, especially when they found out that they were half-breed Iroquis Indians.

When post-war America began there was a hatred for all things 'Not American', including white people that were known in the country and had popular reputations but were now being destroyed by the very government that praised them, all for being a so-called 'Red' or

Communist. The Blacks, Indians, and Japanese were not spared from the country's hatred, but German people in the country didn't seem to have that much of a hard time? It was during these times of hatred that Ling Kwan's power and influence increased, ordering the **Hei-Shou-dang Mafia** to give Wanda and Mildred sanctuary and protection from the people hunting for them at any cost! The sister's sent word up north to the most dangerous people on the Jackson Reservation about their plight, and within weeks a small band of Iroquois killers came and met with some Hei-Shou-dang assassins, forming an allegiance and killing all twenty-seven members of a 'posse' looking to hang Wanda and Mildred, with some women being fatalities during the bloodshed! It was during these 'revenge killings' that Mildred LeeAnn Parker had a dispute with Ling's half-sister LuAn 'Lucy' Kwan and killed her during a duel in the Solace Mountains, then cutting her heart out and eating it over an open campfire with some wild grass and vegetables, then hanging her body from a tree without a 'Christian' burial!

After a couple of days' journey and without leaving James a note, Wanda and Mildred finally made it to the remote place of Solace and were told by people that met them to meet Ling at her home, which was a Chinese styled monastery that had been built into the side of a mountain. When they reached the older, but still ruthless and powerful Ling Kwan's home they were shown in by a young girl that resembled Ling, then were asked to remove their boots and hunting jackets and sit at a table made from the trees of Mont Song, known as the 'council table' and that Ms. Ling would be with them soon. When the still beautiful looking, long gray haired woman entered the room everyone got up and bowed to her then sat down when she sat down, then she greeted Wanda and Mildred like long lost sisters and shared some 'herbal' tea with them while reminiscing about times past. As the evening wore on there was talk from Ling Kwan about an 'eye for an eye' and Mildred having to pay for the death of her half-sister Lucy, when Wanda pulled out a gun and aimed it at Ling and causing Ling's five female assassins to draw their swords and get ready to cut Wanda down to pieces, when Ling held up her hand and they put back their swords and remained quiet. Wanda pleaded with Ling to allow her to bring her sister back home when Ling said to her, "Sometime in the way!" and finished her 'herbal' tea with a stern look at Wanda.

They were allowed to spend the night together as guests of Ms. Ling Kwan and make peace with each other before the sun rose, as Ling

Kwan's traditions did not allow her to kill two brother's or two sister's in the same act of violence, and when the sun rose in the morning Wanda hugged her sister Mildred with deep affection as they both shared tears of remembrance and pain, then Wanda drove off in her beat-up pick-up truck down the long road from Ling Kwan's house in the Solace Mountains, never to see her sister Mildred again.

Part III
Old friends.

When James Rollins returned to the town of Sometime after weeks on the road throughout the midwest as a construction manager for The Federal Projects by the United States, it seemed as if he had missed a decade in the lives of his family as Becky and Dahlia were in Italy and he got word that Wanda and her sister Mildred had went up north, leaving the Atticus Mercantile Company closed indefinitely. After being alone for a couple of days and not hearing from his family, he thought about going to Calumet to see his old girlfriend Kim when a call came to the house, and when he answered the phone it was Ms. Sheila asking to speak with Dahlia? They talked on the phone for hours about their lives growing up in the town of Sometime and the unfortunate death of Big Joe, and how Dahlia 'abandoned' him by going off to Juaniqua County with some girl named April, then Ms. Sheila talking about her time in prison for assaulting a white woman in the town of Shiloh. The next morning was a morning of 'what to do' when a hung over James got another phone call from Ms. Sheila, asking if they could get together for coffee and some drinks in the town of Ineffable, when James told her that he could possibly meet her later that evening?

As he drove through the many towns of the 'anas,' James began to recall all the bad things that happened in each small town he passed until he reached the town of Ineffable and the Gordon Bar, where the statuesque Ms. Sheila was out front waiting. They went into the dimly lit bar that was decorated in Mid-western memorabilia and had a large picture of Officer Thaddeus Baker behind the bar, in respect for being killed in the line of duty, then sat at a booth and began reminiscing about old times and how the both of them were very lonely, and how they missed their inner circle from years ago. It was said by a successful garment merchant in New York that 'dim lighting and cheap fabric' was how you sold merchandise and Ms. Sheila had both, with a cheap fabric dress that hugged her statuesque body and fake jewelry that glittered in the dimly lit bar. Their alcohol induced conversations lasted well into the night and being so far from the town of Sometime, they decided to get a room at the Paradise Motel and look out for each other as James said to Ms. Sheila, " We're old friends!" They drank some more in the motel room and long past emotions began to arise between the two of them, when Ms. Sheila tells James that he was one of the only people that she ever loved, then took her clothes off to take a shower with James following closely behind her into the bathroom.

The steam in the bathroom wasn't the only thing rising, as James and Ms. Sheila told each other how they wanted to 'get with each other' ever since high school and when their shower was done, James sweetened the night by putting two hundred dollars worth of cocaine on a motel mirror as Ms. Sheila draped herself with a yellow silk shirt, then poured James a drink and took two lines of cocaine and dimmed the motel room lights.

The sun is the redeemer of all truths, so it was said in the bible, and when the sun rose between the curtains of the Paradise Motel, James and Ms. Sheila began to feel regret about their night together and immediately started concocting lies and excuses just in case people asked them questions as to their whereabouts, then ordered breakfast from the room service at the Paradise Motel. As they were eating their breakfast they both began to realize that they were alone, because the only people that they ever loved were either gone off to some distant place or were dead! After eating their breakfasts' they were getting themselves ready to leave, and trying to convince themselves that nothing 'happened' between them, when a loud burst of thunder was heard from the sky and within seconds a rain storm descended on the town of Ineffable and canceled everyone's traveling plans for that Saturday afternoon, leaving James and Ms. Sheila to continue their reminiscing about the old days. Since they weren't going anywhere because of the storm, James began putting more cocaine on the motel mirror as Ms. Sheila poured drinks for the both of them, then slipped back into her yellow silk shirt and dimmed the room lights once again.

When the storm had passed and Sunday morning came they both realized that they had to return to their lives, with Ms. Sheila sharing a two-bedroom apartment with a woman that was locked up with her in Shiloh and working as a Social Justice Advocate for the NAACP, and James telling Ms. Sheila that he didn't really have anywhere to go because Dahlia and Becky were in Italy and didn't know when they would be returning, and had no clue where Ms. Wanda Parker Black and her sister Mildred went? They walked out into the afternoon air from the storm that had passed and before getting into their separate cars, they passionately kissed in the parking lot and shared one last memory with each other and before leaving, Ms. Sheila told James not to be a stranger for long because they were old friends!

Part IV.
Death to Barabbas.

The young Gloria Loren proved to be a loyal and resourceful liaison to Becky both in Italy and while she was abroad, when Becky made arrangements from France to have Gloria hired as her personal assistant and managing most of her affairs. She was a most gracious host to Dahlia and with the help of Barabbas, Dahlia got to experience the things she dreamed about while going to 'patch of dirt university' and reading books about archeological expeditions and ***Dust tracks on a road*** by her favorite writer. Since her stay in Italy, Dahlia had not heard from her mother or James and with Becky playing in France, the only people close to her were Gloria and her cat Barabbas, making Dahlia think about Juaniqua County with April Carrington and not wanting to return to the town of Sometime?

Besides her duties as Becky's personal assistant and helping Dahlia speak Italian and keep her from getting lost on sight-seeing walks, she had her hands full with keeping her cat Barabbas out of trouble. There were **Wanted** posters in certain towns for the cat's arrest for killing chickens on people's farms and stealing jewelry from rich old women, while posing as a lost, helpless cat and once taken in by the gullible women, Barabbas would steal their jewelry and bury it somewhere in the Italian mountains. The cat was accused of murder when the owner of a cat named Pontius killed a man, claiming self-defense in court because the man was going to kill Pontius and Barabbas in the back of a fish market and accused the two cats of stealing fish and trying to blame an innocent cat named Susej for the crime. In some small Italian villages and towns the people became increasingly upset with the cat's antics, calling for 'Morte Barabbas' or death to Barabbas and causing Gloria to make plans to get her cat out of the country!

With Becky feeling lonely over in France and wanting to get

Barabbas out of the country, Gloria made arrangements for Dahlia to stay with her aunt Sophia in a town called Burano in Venice, hoping that her aunt and Dahlia would read Zora Neale Hurston books together to occupy their time, then booking a flight to France to see Becky and get Barabbas out of town!

While maintaining a 'goddess among the people' persona and dominating the women's basketball league around the world, Becky was exhausted and wanted the comfort of her closest friends but found out from a letter from Sara that Rebeca was in a convent, caused by a nervous breakdown after the Eden Winter game in Kansas. It was sad for her to hear about her best friend Rebeca being put in another institution, but glad to hear that Sara Blackfoot was still alive and looking forward to the arrival of Gloria and Barabbas to cheer her up! On the way to the airport her aunt Sophia provided extra security for her, as many people along the route to the airport and around the small towns held up signs reading 'Morte Barabbas,' until she got safely on a plane to France to meet Becky. A day or two had passed since Gloria and Barabbas boarded the flight to France and as Becky prepared for another tournament game, the television news came on in the girl's locker room about the disappearance of flight 107 that was bound for France over the North Atlantic Ocean. After hearing the news on the television, Becky immediately went into her gym bag and looked in her itinerary and read '*Gloria and Barabbas arrive in France flight 107,*' and when a television reporter mentioned that the villainous cat Barabbas was among those killed in the plane crash; some of her teammates and other people in the locker room began cheering 'Morte Barabbas'!

Part V
Postcards from Italy.

With the death of Gloria and her beloved cat over the North Atlantic Ocean, Gloria's aunt Sophia grieved with Dahlia and offered her all the comforts of Italy while she was staying there, and while drinking wine with Dahlia in her Villa in Burano behind the Italian Mountains she told Dahlia which 'leading men' in her movies she hated, and the ones that were homosexuals but had wives and children. Their stories about 'movie stars' and discussing books by Zora Neale Hurston kept their minds off of Gloria's passing, as Dahlia thought about Becky returning to Italy after her tournament in France and flying across the same ocean that killed Gloria and Barabbas, and with aunt Sophia's wine induced advice, Dahlia decided not to return to the town of Sometime but stay in Italy with her daughter.

When Becky returned from France and met by her mother who needed no sign in the airport, they left for Becky's loft apartment without hardly speaking to each other as the cab drove through the ancient streets where she lived, and as the cab approached her apartment with faded 'Wanted' signs for the death of Barabbas still nailed to telephone poles, Becky asked her mother what her plans were before she left for some time?

"Sometime! I hope to God that I never set foot on that soil again!"

"What about Dad and grandma Wanda, and great aunt Mildred and the store, who's going to look after those things?"

"Those 'things' will take care of themselves Becky LeeAnn, besides, I'm not in love with James anymore and I have a feeling that he's fucking my best friend, Ms. Sheila!"

"Lord in Christ, my friend and her cat just perished over the ocean and I just found out that Rebeca is in a convent, now you want to ditch going back to Sometime and travel around the world with me?"

"Yes! My dreams are going to die if I go back to Sometime just because a girl and a cat died in a plane crash! I'll let everyone know how were doing in Italy by sending them postcards."

"Well, I guess I'm stuck with you for a while, how's your Italian?"

"Molto bene mia figlia! I'll send postcards to let everyone know what's going on with us over here, I told you we were going to have a nice time in Italy!"

"I'm glad you're here ma, as much as I hate the town of Sometime I miss it, sometime? By the way, you can't carry a gun around and shoot people if they upset you!"

"I found that out in Burano with Mrs. Loren when a man saw me reading my book and called Zora Neale Hurston a 'Communist Nigger,' so I pulled out my gun and took a shot at him in the town square! Mrs. Loren came and bailed me out and reminded me that I wasn't in the midwest!"

"Lord in Christ, try to behave yourself while you're with me in Italy!"

"I'll get myself settled and get started on those postcards, that fucking Ms. Sheila!"

Once she got settled in and started feeling comfortable with her daughter and her new surroundings, Dahlia wrote a small letter on a postcard to James to let him know that she would be staying with Becky for about a year, and to check on her mother and great-aunt Mildred and watch out over the store. When James Rollins got the postcard from Italy he was shocked, but relieved that Dahlia would not be coming home soon as he was making good money running The Atticus Mercantile Store by himself, with the occasional assistance of Ms. Sheila. He had gotten word from people in the 'anas' that Wanda had survived a bear attack, but that her great-aunt Mildred wasn't so fortunate and that Wanda had retreated into the Solace mountains, to grieve her sister's death and kill the bear that had killed her sister in the Iriquios tradition.

Although he was a fornicator and never stayed loyal to anything in his life except himself and Big Joe, James Rollins was responsible and wrote back to Dahlia and Becky about the goings on in the 'anas,' and when Dahlia received the letter from James about a bear killing aunt Mildred and her mother in isolation in the Solace Mountains, Dahlia felt a sense of relief but didn't tell Becky about what happened to her beloved great-aunt Mildred. While Becky tried to relax after a grueling tournament in France, where she won the MVP of the Women's European League and a championship for Team Italia, she got the addressee of the convent that Rebeca was staying in from Sara and wrote the both of them small letters from postcards she collected from around the world. A few months went by as Becky bonded with her mother in Italy and got ready to travel around the world again, when she got letters from Rebeca and Sara thanking her for her postcards from Italy and asking when she would be coming back to the states?

Chapter IX
The Relevance of Time

Since the times of sending postcards and letters across the oceans many things had changed, as Dahlia had fulfilled her dreams of archeological expeditions in Italy and Egypt then returned to Sometime to tend to her ailing mother Wanda, only to be involved in a love triangle with James and Ms. Sheila. While playing for Team Italia around the world Becky had amassed a small fortune and along with her endorsements, she considered retiring after nearly ten years of world travel and the wear and tear that was happening to her body was starting to catch up to her. In the Villa that was a gift from her 'new found' aunt Sophia in Burano she read all things American, especially about a slow footed white kid from Indiana taking the NBA by storm and winning a championship with an Irish basketball team in Boston, and letters from Sara, who lived mysteriously up in the Canadian Mountains, about Rebeca leaving the Convent of Mary Magdalene and staying with her grandmother.

She was alone in Italy and contemplating retiring after her final game of the season against the women's German team, known as the "Frauen auf Nazi's' or Women Nazi's because of their physical play and hatred for most things black or Jewish! The game was to be played in Nuremberg, Germany and the cold weather was just right for certain players, especially for the German team's roughest and toughest player named Edna Vinter, who grew up in the Bavarian Alps killing animals with her bare hands and chopping wood in the cold while half dressed. The stormy flight from Italy to Germany made Becky more nervous than she usually was, but once she landed in Germany the word was already in the newspapers how Edna Vinter was waiting for her and going to end her 'Goddess among the people' reign in basketball! The six-foot, six-inch and one hundred and ninety-five pound Aryan even went so far as to mention to the newspapers how she had talked to someone from Wichita, Kansas, telling her how Becky Rollins Black was a 'bastard nigger child' born from alcoholic 'niggers' in the midwest, and was best friends with a girl who killed her father because he was half German! She was holed up and isolated in her hotel room in Nuremberg, reading in the newspapers what Edna Vinter had said about her and her family and best friend Rebeca and became enraged with an Iroquois spirit of revenge! A fierce winter storm blew through Nuremberg and the game was postponed for two days, leaving Becky alone in her hotel room to remember her times on Aianta cliff with Rebeca and Sara, and 'why' Rebeca killed her father! She paced the room while remembering going up for a lay-up on a crate in 'the park,' then waking up in a hospital because the back of her head was nearly split open by landing on a rock, and the nasty things Eden Winter had said to Rebeca during their game in Kansas, which caused her to have a nervous breakdown and be sent to a convent! While the inclement weather continued and the fervor for the game increased, Becky got a telegram from Rebeca that read how she was staying with her Grandma Dean and had been feeling poorly but wishing Becky good luck in her game, leaving her with the message of 'why' she was in Germany and all their friendship had endured, then ending with 'Remember Eden Winter and kick that German bitch's ass!!! Love Rebeca!

Her restless night was over and the sun shined through the curtains in her room, then the phone rang and when she answered it she was informed that the game would be played at seven in the evening then was abruptly hung up on, only fueling her Iroquois blood after reading the telegram from Rebeca the night before. A car came and picked her up to take her to a high school gymnasium for practice with her teammates, and when she arrived the German paparazzi were taking pictures and asking her rude questions in German until the police led them away and she could practice with some quiet. In between breaks during practice Becky would read the telegram that Rebeca sent her over and over and while keeping her distance from her teammates, some of them wondered if she was going to retire after the game and if her parents and best friend were really as bad as the newspapers printed? After practice and with a few hours before the game Becky went off by herself to a wooded area behind the team facility, going into an Iroquois state of mind as if a close person had died until a few of her teammates went to get her and thought she had lost her mind, as she sat by a small campfire and was mumbling incoherent words that her teammates never heard before. When the game finally got underway Becky seemed depressed and wilting like a tall flower under the bright light of the sun, with Edna Vinter taunting her and a few people in the stands holding up signs that read 'Go home nigger' and 'Drunk black monkey' which made Becky cry and feel like the only black person in the world. The first half of the game was dominated by Edna Vinter and the German women's team, as she bullied and elbowed Becky to the ribs and head and knocked her half unconscious with a hard foul that sent Becky to the locker room. A book written by Charles Dickens a century ago was named 'A tale of two cities' and the game played between Germany and Italy, or between Becky and Edna Vinter was just that, as Becky returned to the game in the second half and became a one woman wrecking crew as she scored 53 points and grabbed 17 rebounds along with 10 assists, and elbowing Edna Vinter in the ribs so hard that she broke two of her ribs and had to be carried off the court by the 'Frauen auf Nazis,' as the signs people were holding against her slowly came down or were being torn up!

   The game against Germany in Nuremberg was televised across the globe like telephone wires and with Becky winning another championship trophy, she thanked the Lord and her teammates on national television for the victory, along with thanking Rebeca for her telegram of inspiration and telling the people that were assembled that she wasn't retiring from basketball, causing those that held up signs of hatred not too long ago to applaud her and shout 'Viva Becky' as she left the cold gymnasium in Nuremberg, Germany.

Part I
Till death do us part.

With the triumph in Germany and changing the way that many people in Europe thought about blacks in the world, but some people still having problems getting along with Jews, Becky became an unofficial Ambassador of Goodwill by the United States and continued to play basketball around the world until 1985, when a knee injury took her out of a game at the beginning of the season. While she recuperated in her Villa in Burano she got letters from her mother Dahlia, writing to her about Grandmother Wanda's declining health which was mainly due to the death of her sister Mildred than of old age, and how her father James Rollins ran off with another woman that wasn't Ms. Sheila. She got encouragement from some of her teammates to rehabilitate her left knee and hoped that she would come back to Team Italia, because she was the best woman basketball player in the world and without her endorsements, the team would be just another bad team in the European Women's League and they would never make the money they were making at the time.

She sent money to her mother to care for Wanda Black but told her in letters that she could only do so much, because she had no plans of returning to the town of Sometime regardless of who died or ran off with who, but was only thinking of rehabilitating her injured knee and playing another season. The fact that her father ran off with another woman didn't bother her that much, as she remembered father's when she was growing up and most of them being 'Pezzo di merda' or 'Pieces of shit' and continued to send her mother things from Italy. During her ten year basketball career in Europe she won 5 World Championships, 6 League MVP's, 7 Rebounding honors and was Defensive Player of the Year 4 times, but never played on the U. S. Women's Olympic Team because of what happened to Ms. Sheila and how she was denied her dreams because of the racism in the country. It would take a year of strenuous rehabilitation for Becky's injured knee to mend, and at thirty-three years old the doctors were not optimistic about her recovery or comeback to play basketball like she used to, when her questions about retiring and returning to the midwest were answered when she got a letter from Sara Blackfoot about the condition of their friend Rebeca?

The letter that Becky received from Sara was about Rebeca being 'released' from The Convent of Mary Magdalene after her nervous breakdown, then trying to adapt with the amplified world around her and going so far as to get a part-time job at Aurora University. She taught psychology classes but quit because of constant questions about her being the woman that killed her father when she was younger, and if she knew the famous basketball player Becky Black Rollins and the Indian woman outlaw in the Canadian Territories known as 'Black Sara'? In the letter, Sara explained how her family was involved in a 'territorial' dispute and when they went to reclaim their property, four people were killed during the conflict while trying to attack her and her husband Quint along with their three children! Becky read how Sara was being blamed for the killings and wanted by the police from the territories, then decided to leave with her daughter to get a fair deal in Sometime and also see Rebeca, who was trying to quietly spend her time reading and writing at her Grandma Dean's home in Fairmont. Sara also explained in the letter how Rebeca went into a depression when her doctor discovered that she had ovarian cancer and didn't have much time to live, which hastened her decision to go see her! The tear filled letter from Sara described how Rebeca felt the friendship between the three of them was like a marriage and 'Till death do us part,' and praying that they could be there in her final times on earth? After Becky finished reading Sara's letter written in broken Indian and English at least three times she tearfully began packing her belongings, ready to leave her Villa in Burano and make the long journey back to the midwest to see her dying friend, and to find out what all the 'outlaw' business was regarding Sara!

Part II
Gone to Kansas!

It was a beautiful day in the town of Burano as the tomatoes and other vegetables began sprouting in peoples' gardens, and with the freshness that is Italy and light breezes throughout the town, Becky left a message with a teammate over the phone that she had decided to retire, and a note in her hotel room thanking her teammates for their help and support over the years but decided to go to Kansas! She was going to Kansas to confront Eden Winter about the things she said in the European newspapers, especially about how her parents were 'alcoholic midwestern niggers' and the other nasty things she said about Rebeca that caused her to have a nervous breakdown. With a fire and vengeance burning within her competitive black and Iroquis soul, Becky left under the cover of darkness and boarded a flight to The United States, and the almost ten thousand miles across The Atlantic Ocean before she could get close to Kansas. When her teammates read her note most of them had no idea where Kansas was or if it even existed, and told the Italian people that Becky had gone on a sabbatical somewhere in the Canadian mountains, to a remote place called 'CanSas'!

She arrived at John F. Kennedy Airport in New York and not wanting to draw attention to herself, she sat on a bench so her height would not give her away and paid a man $50 dollars to buy her a plane ticket to Wichita, Kansas, and when she got her first-class ticket from the stranger she immediately boarded the plane without being recognized, then ordered a bottle of Champagne and two Rum and Cokes from the airline stewardess while the plane was getting ready to take off for Kansas. During her flight she spent most of her time drinking Rum and

Cokes and reading the letter that Sara had sent her, trying to figure out how Sara became an outlaw and remembering the night Rebeca shot and killed her father Tyrus, which made Becky wanting to see Rebeca even more and Eden Winter even less. The flight landed in Kansas and by the time Becky got off the plane slightly intoxicated, people were beginning to recognize the tall and beautiful world famous basketball player, who also did commercials on television that were broadcast around the world for any American family with a television set to see.

With some yokels beginning to stare at her and asking for Polaroid pictures, Becky got a cab from the airport and told the driver to take her to a car dealership and once she got there she tipped the cab driver $50 dollars, then spoke with an awestruck salesman and bought a $10 thousand dollar black BMW and after getting directions and taking a Polaroid with the salesman, she found a motel to stay in for the night so she could wake up early the next morning and find out where Eden Winter lived. The morning in Dawson County brought rain and the gossip of a famous guest, as people were gathering more than usual at Victoria's Diner and awaiting the arrival of the tall celebrity that came into their town, so they could gawk and take pictures of her when she came into the only place to eat in town. When the large clock on the church in the town that dictated everyone's movements and daily routines struck noon, they all paused and waited for the tall, statuesque black woman to come out of the Algonquin Motel and walk a few yards to the Victoria Diner to sit down and eat. Becky entered the diner and felt the eyes of Kansas on her as she sat in a booth and ordered a breakfast of scrambled eggs and a side of toast with coffee, when certain people started mumbling loudly about the international person in the diner that 'may' have been involved in the death of Tyrus Van Meter? It was only when a young girl and her dog told everyone in the diner to leave Becky alone and to let her eat in peace, calling the men in the diner 'goat raping hillbillies' and the women 'fat door mats' and her dog protecting everything she said!

Becky appreciated the young girl speaking out on her behalf and asked the girl and her dog to join her for breakfast and when they did, Becky began to think about Gloria and Barabbas in Italy and within a few minutes she asked the free-spirited girl to be her guide to find a woman in Kansas named Eden Winter, which she agreed to do with the stipulation that she could bring her black Rottweiler dog named Judas on the trip? Before Becky could finish her breakfast and ignore what the people in the Victoria Diner were saying about her, the young girl introduced herself as Virginia Otoe Taylor and told Becky that Otoe was Indian for 'Blue River,' then ordered a bunch of sausages to go for Judas and told Becky that regardless of her celebrity that there was still hatred that runs 'like roots in a tree,' and that they should leave Dawson County for friendlier environments. Becky continued to calmly eat her breakfast as other people were arguing around her, then told the pretty, Goth looking girl and her dog that she knew all about the 'hatred of roots' and not 'just in trees,' and had a car across the parking lot at the Algonquin Motel and could use a hand getting her things together before they left. Virginia whispered in her dog's ear and now Judas understood that he was going to be the protector of both women, and when the check came from the awestruck, nervous young waitress holding out a pen for Becky's autograph, she signed the bill 'From Sometime' and left the waitress a $20 dollar tip with Virginia taking the bag of sausages and Judas walking behind them like he was protecting a royal detail as they left the Victoria Diner. As the motley crew of Becky and her two new friends walked across the parking lot in the rain towards the motel a woman in the diner said, "What a sight, a tall nigger woman with a junkie girl and a loyal, betraying dog by her side. I've never seen such a sight in all my days since I lived in Kansas!"

When they got to the Algonquin Motel they gathered the things that Becky wanted to take, with Virginia occasionally interrupting her because of the beautiful things she had and Judas sniffing and barking at every little irritation while they packed. A crowd gathered outside The Algonquin Motel as Becky and her two damp friends got everything into her BMW, when the woman from the Victoria Diner came out and told them that they weren't going anywhere because she was 'kin' to Tyrus Van Meter! Victoria quieted Judas from his aggressive movements towards the woman and pulled out a gun and told everyone to back up, which they did as Victoria and Judas got into the car when Becky told the woman, "Your piece of shit 'kin' had it coming, and I'm only in this redneck shithole to find a person that troubled my friend!"

They got into Becky's car and drove off from the stupefied crowd and headed to the main road, with Victoria and Judas looking over a map that she carried in her back pocket in case of emergencies, so she could find the quickest way out of Dawson County and Becky driving down the highway, with the wind blowing through her shoulder length hair and taking a sip of scotch from her flask and listening to Pavarotti on her cassette player. After driving several miles and Judas eating the sausages that Victoria gave him, she began to get irritable and sweating and asked Becky to pull over to the truck stop off the highway, which she did at 30 miles an hour and Victoria asking her for $50 dollars to get information about where Eden Winter lived. When Becky gave Victoria the $50 dollars to go into the truck stop diner, she left the car with Judas following behind her and told Becky she wouldn't be long. About half an hour had passed since Victoria and Judas left the car and Becky was getting nervous, as she continued to listen to Pavarotti and take sips from her flask and checking her pocket book to make sure her gun was there, when Victoria and Judas came out of the truck stop diner like giddy school kids and got back into the car.

The sun was setting behind the trees off the highway and driving on dark roads was no longer becoming an option, when Judas barked at the map and Victoria told Becky to get off at the next exit to stay at a motel for the night, which Becky did and pulled into the Shudder Inn and gave Victoria $100 dollars to give to the desk clerk for two rooms for the night. After checking in they drove a few paces and pulled up to their rooms, with Victoria and Judas helping Becky into room #345 with her belongings and sitting for a moment, to rest and tell Becky about her and Judas' journey through the midwest. She sat in Becky's motel room and smoked cigarettes and drank a nip of Bacardi, while Becky rubbed ointment on her injured knee and drank a glass of wine while listening to an old Patsy Cline song on the motel radio. Victoria told Becky how she ran away from home with Judas because her alcoholic white father would abuse her and her mother Claire, who was an Osage Indian woman from Kansas. Becky began to listen to her more intently when she mentioned 'abused by her father' and thought about Rebeca, and the never ending cycle of abuse and why Victoria didn't just kill her father?

Victoria continued to talk about her rough and tumble journey through life, then told Becky she found out from the truck stop diner where Eden Winter lived and after writing the name of the town on a piece of paper, she became sweaty and agitated and got her key from Becky to go to her room and telling Becky before she left, "You're the greatest thing I ever saw in my life! You remind me of my older sister Lynnette before she was killed, but not as tall!" She retreated to her room #346 and immediately turned on the radio and her a Waylon Jennings song as she got comfortable, then got all the necessary things out of her bag to 'cook-up' the $50 dollars' worth of heroin that she scored from the truck stop diner and telling Judas to watch the door, then shooting the heroin into her pretty Goth troubled veins while listening to a Waylon Jennings outlaw song.

Part III
A short conversation with Mrs. Winter.

Becky read the addressee on the paper that Victoria left and couldn't believe what she read, that Eden Winter actually lives in a town called Winter? The note also read that the town of Winter was about 75 miles heading towards Missouri, and that Eden Winter came from a large family that were not partial to outsiders. There weren't to many people that knew where the six-feet, five-inch tall, world famous black woman basketball and endorsement star was, as Becky drank some "herbal tea' that her grandmother Wanda and great-aunt Mildred gave to her as a present for her parade, along with a handmade 'peace pipe' and her 'herbs' she brought from Italy. She began to remember all the things that she had experienced in her life to get to this point, in the middle of nowhere Kansas, and how Dahlia and her grandmother were doing back in Sometime, and her teammates back in Italy and Mrs. Loren? As the night settled in at the Shudder Inn and a heavy wind blew through open windows, the blowing motel curtains in the rooms made everyone in them realize 'why' they were in the middle of nowhere Kansas, and Becky preparing to drive towards Missouri to confront Eden Winter for the things that she said, even to the 'Freuen auf ' bitches in Europe, and after that she would continue to drive through Missouri into Indiana.

The winds from the night before at the Shudder Inn settled as a milky white sun rose into the clouds, causing a grayness to the morning of Becky's obsessive early rise, when Victoria and Judas welcomed themselves into her room with breakfast from the kitchen at the Shudder Inn, telling a half dressed, obsessed black woman ready to go to Missouri how her and Judas got the breakfast because she went into the kitchen to complain about the food and when she did, Judas scared everyone in the kitchen and they left with the breakfasts' made for other people, and thirty sausages for Judas. Becky finished getting dressed as Judas sniffed around nervously and Victoria not knowing what was going to happen her, when Becky asked her to be her guide like 'Pocahontas' to the town of Winter and through Missouri, when Victoria and Judas started jumping and barking up and down with excitement and about to go to the next room and gather their things, when Victoria turned and told Becky "I hate Missouri, and Kansas not so much!," then left with Judas following closely behind her and took a much needed hot shower with Judas to wash away the road and trouble that had followed them.

After the mid-afternoon shower that cleansed away some of the sins of her and Judas, Victoria put on a long black shirt and jeans with black Chuck Taylor canvas high top sneakers and wrapped a black bandana around Judas' thick neck, then gathered up her things and walked next door as the wind dried her waist length black hair and teary blue eyes and saw Becky coming out of her motel room, looking like a Black Panther from the 1970's dressed in all black with dark sunglasses and a black beret she got from Italy. They got into Becky's black BMW and took off from the parking lot of the Shudder Inn, with Ma and Pa Shudder looking out the front office window at the tall black woman dressed in all black and a troubled girl with her dog driving in an expensive car when Mrs. Shutter said, "I've never seen anything like that in all my days living in Kansas, and I pray for that girl and her dog!" The drive to the town of Winter was not as long as Becky thought, as Victoria and Judas looked over her crumpled map with circles around certain towns and Judas barking at every exit that should have been taken, when the town of Winter showed up on the map and Judas barked quietly for Becky to get off the road.

Becky drove into the desolate town of Winter, Kansas and thought that nobody lived in the town, when a stranger on the road pointed towards a big house off in the distance and told Becky that the Winter family lived up the road. When she pulled up to the house that the stranger had pointed out to her, she began to lose her hatred for Eden Winter but still wanted to confront her about the things she said and did to Rebeca, while Victoria prepared another shot of heroin in the backseat of Becky's car and Judas watching everything from strangers. She got out of her car and stood for a minute in front of the Winter family home, when a person tending plants and flowers on the porch pulled out a gun on Becky and causing Judas to leave the car to protect Becky, when a heroin high Victoria said two words to Judas that made him cautious and docile. Becky got out of her car and cautiously approached the elderly woman that was attending the garden on the porch, asking her if she knew Eden Winter or her whereabouts? The elderly woman stopped tending to her little path of garden and invited

Becky into her home for tea, which Becky accepted and began to smell the air that she hated from Kansas as Victoria read a book from Zora Neale Hurston about being black in America.

"Hello mam, my name's Becky from the town of Sometime, would you happen to know a woman by the name of Eden Winter?"

"Yes I would, she's my daughter! My name is Eileen Winter and I'm the mother of thirteen children, what's your business with Eden?"

"I mean no disrespect to you Mrs. Winter, but I traveled a long way to speak with your daughter about bad feelings!"

"I remember you! You were the tall black girl on the television that beat Wichita State for the National Championship and caused a lot of problems for my daughter."

"I wanted to talk with Edna and ask her 'why' she said the things she said about my family, and the nasty things she said about my friend Rebeca!"

"Did your friend kill her father?"

"Yes, Mrs. Winter…"

"Then we are almost even in the tolls of death, as my daughter Eden killed herself with a hunting rifle up in the Indiana Mountains! She went up there to get away from the embarrassment of losing to you and what happened in Europe, but it was told by many people from the 'anas' that she was killed by some Indian outlaw woman?"

"So, Eden Winter is dead?"

Yes she is, like most of my children!"

"If you don't mind me asking, what are the names of your children?"

"The names of my children are Edward, Elijah, Elizabeth, Elma, Elmore, Elisa, Eden, Emory, Ethan, Ezekiel, Eileen, Elwood, and Eli, with most of them dying from the horrors of war or diseases! I have six children left on God's earth and many grandchildren spread throughout the parts of the world, and a granddaughter left by Eden."

"Eden Winter has a daughter?"

"Yes, she does, even though she got her head blown off in the Indiana Mountains! She lives with her aunt Elisa and her husband somewhere in a town called Sometime."

"Sometime, that's where I'm from and going to visit my friend!"

"Well, tell your friend that my daughter Eden had no hard feelings against her, even though that girl did kill her father, but she just hated people from the town of Sometime!"

It began to rain heavily as Becky left the home of Mrs. Winter after her short conversion with her and felt a sense of relief and sadness, knowing that Eden Winter was dead but had a child where she was from? She got back into her car with a sleeping Victoria and Judas in the back seat and became agitated with them, asking them why they couldn't stay awake for an hour while she prayed not to get killed by the old woman that was tending to her garden on the porch? They apologized to Becky with half nods and silent barks as she drove off to Missouri which was almost 400 miles to Sometime, then realized as she drove down another dark highway, that Judas had not eaten any of the thirty sausages that Victoria had gotten for him at the Shudder Inn?

Part IV
The trials of Pocahontas.

The drive through Missouri began to take a toll on the pretty young Goth girl from Osage County, as Victoria 'scored' heroin from every truck stop and diner they stopped off at, while Becky began to wonder 'why' Victoria had scratch marks and bumps on her arms and was coughing all the time? The news around the country began to talk about a deadly virus called AIDS, which was contracted by homosexuals having sex with each other or by intravenous drug use, dispelling the myth that the disease came from vampire monkeys in Africa that somehow came to America and started biting white people in their necks. She got 'dope sick' with every town they traveled through and Judas was becoming more irritable, as the roads and highways began to wear on Becky she took Virginia to a courthouse for shooting a man in Dawson County. When Virginia went to court for various offenses in the town of Knowaire, Missouri, the judge of the town was named Roosevelt Hannibal and sentenced her to thirty days in jail, pending a trial and the execution of her dog Judas! Becky came to realize that Virginia wasn't using heroin for a sports injury, like she saw with women players 'popping' morphine and painkiller pills like they were taking vitamins, but for a pain deep inside of her, like the kind of pain that Rebeca has to carry around with her every day.

The trial of Virginia Otoe Taylor began on a rainy Thursday morning, with some people from Dawson County on the jury, in particular the woman that confronted her, Judas, and Becky in the parking lot at the Shudder Inn, and her fate seemed inevitable and the execution of her dog Judas. The prosecution against Virginia and her dog Judas charged them with robbery and willful theft, maleficence, vagrancy, rude and lascivious behavior, attempted murder, and going so far as to charge the both of them of betraying Jesus Christ, when the woman from the Victoria Diner got up in the courtroom and yelled, "Crucify them!" While the jury convened before they rendered their inevitable verdict against Virginia and Judas, Becky used her worldwide celebrity and told Judge Roosevelt Hannibal in private the trials of Virginia Otoe Taylor, or as she referred to her as 'My Pocahontas' and how she was guiding her through Kansas with the help of Judas. Judge Roosevelt Hannibal was from a proud Southern family and strident upholder of the law, but when Becky posted five thousand dollars bond in cash in the judges hands and had a Polaroid taken with him, Virginia and Judas were released within an hour out a back door from the courthouse with Becky waiting in her black BMW, and as they drove off discreetly from the courthouse and the judge showing his Polaroid of Becky to his staff, the woman from the Victoria Diner stood outside the courthouse and saw them driving off and shouting at them, "Matthew 27 verse 9, Judas had betrayed Jesus, but when he learned that Jesus had been sentenced to death, he was sorry for what he had done! And that Goddamn betraying dog will be the death of you all!"

Part V
No Alohas.

It's almost 400 miles from Missouri to Indiana and Becky knew she had her hands full with Virginia and Judas, with several towns and roads in between to reach the town of Sometime and thinking about Rebeca's health, and how her mother and grandmother were fairing, when Virginia and Judas looked over her crumpled map in the back seat and told Becky to pull off at the next exist for the town of Solomon, with Judas barking in agreement. She pulled into the Velvet Inn and did the usual routine with Virginia and Judas by giving them money to check them into the motel, and while they went to the front desk to sign in, Becky checked her leather valise that had almost two hundred thousand dollars in cash and her pocket book to make sure she had her gun. She sat in the car smoking a cigarette and listening to a cassette of Tchaikovsky while thinking about the 'Trial of Pocahontas,' and how she just walked into a judge's chambers with a gun in her pocket book? After a few minutes Virginia and Judas came skipping out of the front desk office, with Virginia giggling the keys between her stubby little fingers and Judas following closely beside her. They got adjoining rooms and as usual Virginia and Judas helped carry Becky's belongings into her room, as Becky brought in her 'personal luggage' and went to the phone in her room to check her messages from Italy while Virginia sat in the middle of the room, and Judas walking around sniffing everything and rubbing up against Becky while she was on the phone.

After being on the phone for a while and telling some people from Italy that she was officially retired and would deal with her financial matters later, she looked up and saw a lonely young girl sitting in the middle of the motel floor and grabbed a bottle of scotch and a pack of cigarettes, then went in the living-room and sat on the couch next to Virginia and poured two glasses of scotch and gave one to Virginia and a cigarette. The country tunes from the motel radio played into the night, as Virginia and Becky talked about their lives growing up in the midwest and how an uncle had given her heroin when she was sixteen years old to help her with her leg pain, and how he tried to molest her and stole money from him because he was a licensed physician. Becky enjoyed listening to her as Judas sat around like a loyal disciple, never having eaten the thirty sausages that were given to him at the Shudder Inn and Virginia throwing them in front of the place as they left the town after her trial.

"Ms. Becky, why did you travel all the way from Italy to come to Kansas and Missouri?"

"I have a sick friend and I want to be there when she dies, or I couldn't live with myself. That's why I left Italy to come to these God forsaken places!"

"She must be really important to you, I wish I had friends like that?"

"Well, you got me and Judas, that's a start!"

"It hasn't been the same for me since my sister Lynnette was killed in a car accident while driving in a storm, and people have been trying to kill me and Judas ever since we left Osage County, my poor mother Claire, I wonder how she's fairing these days?"

"Do you ever think about going back home, maybe just to see your mother?"

"I'll never go back to that place, whether I'm dead or alive!"

"I'll take you as far as the Missouri border and give you some money to help you and Judas, but I have personal affairs to tend to when I get to Sometime."

"When our time comes to part ways, they'll be no Alohas! I hate hellos and good-byes with people, because I never see them again?"

"Virginia, whatever happens from here till Indiana, you 'stay in the buggy' and try not to die on me! Christ in Jesus, can you people stop dying on me!"

"I'll do my best to 'stay in the buggy,' and keep Judas out of trouble until we reach Sometime!"

"We, in Sometime? This isn't France!"

The Missouri sun is like no other, for when it rises it scorches everything under its dry plains, even the shadows of little creatures, and the Missouri sun was beginning to scorch Virginia's addiction to heroin as it baked within her body, and Judas trying to remain loyal to her. Becky gave her some money and dropped her and Judas off at the Mall of Solomon and told them she would pick them up in an hour, as she had some letters to mail at the post office and had to meet a man about Sara's whereabouts in the midwest? Virginia and Judas walked around the mall full of people and felt like convicted criminals, as Judas strutted apprehensively beside Virginia as if he no longer knew her. She bought a Larry Bird T-shirt with him looking like a chicken with a basketball and another pair of black canvas Chuck Taylor's, when she was confronted by two white men in the Mall of Solomon about Becky's whereabouts and the outlaw Sara Blackfoot, and 'why' she was in the town of Solomon? They took her out to the underground parking lot of the Mall and sexually violated her in their car, while her dog sniffed around as if nothing was happening, then gave her a bag of heroin for her troubles along with a black eye and a mouth full of blood!

When Becky picked them up at the Mall of Solomon, Virginia was in bad shape and told Becky that she didn't tell the two white men that beat her up and raped her anything about her and Sara's whereabouts! This made Becky tighten the grip on her .38 Caliber gun in her pocket book even more, and to get Virginia and Judas back at the Velvet Inn as soon as possible after sending letters to the Post Office in the town of Solomon, then meeting a man that knew about Sara's condition while she traveled to the town of Sometime with her daughter earlier in the day.

The sun is a rapacious entity and all things on earth owe to it, as do the souls of Godless Philistines, when Virginia and Judas took their wounded souls into the room next to Becky's and tried to finish their betrayal to her? She spent a brutal and restless night thinking about Rebeca and where Sara was in the midwest, and what to do with the troubled guide she called 'Pocahontas' and her betraying dog Judas? When she finally fell asleep in her room at the Velvet Inn under the sedation of the painkillers she was taking for her knee injury, and the stress from her mother Dahlia and grandmother Wanda in Sometime, Virginia healed her wounds and problems trying to slept by shooting some of the heroin that the two white men gave her at the mall.

Becky and Judas tended to Virginia as best they could at the Velvet Inn to help her overcome her rape and beating, while Judas kept watch and thought about the thirty sausages that were thrown away and Becky tending to Victoria. While putting cold towels on Victoria's feverish body, Becky thought about how Eden Winter put a hunting rifle around her mouth and shot her brains out, knowing she had a child that lived in Sometime? A few days had passed and Victorias' spirits picked up and she was ready to move on to the next town, when Becky told her that she had to meet a man about where Sara was and would be back soon, and as soon as Becky left, Victoria prepared her "kit' to shoot more of the heroin she got from the two men that raped and beat her. When Becky returned from meeting the man in town about Sara's situation, Victoria was ready to leave the Velvet Inn and told her that people were coming to kill them and that they should make an exodus from the town of Solomon, when Becky gathered a half overdosed Virginia and put her into the car with the help of Judas. She gathered up all her belongs like she was catching a flight to Italy and drove to the nearest town named Koto, and when she asked Virginia to look at her crumpled map to find the nearest exist and when she didn't respond or hear Judas barking in agreement, she pulled over to the side of an unlit road.

   Becky turned the inside light on in her car and when she turned around to the back seat, she could see that the Goth looking girl was paler than usual and reached her long black arms around the back seat, grabbing Virginia by the neck and wrist to check for a pulse?

   She spent little time grieving and drove to the nearest bus station to put her on a bus to see her mother Claire, and once she got to the Exodus Bus Terminal in the town of Solomon, Judas ran out the back seat of the car and disappeared from Becky's sight. She went into the bus terminal and purchased a one way ticket for Virginia Otoe Taylor to Osage County to the care of Ms. Claire Taylor, and when she went to put

Virginia on the bus in a wheelchair, she saw Judas hanging from a tree across from the parking lot with a sign around his neck that read 'Betrayer'! Before she had Virginia put on the bus by two attendants she wrote a note and put it in Virginia's black Chuck Taylor sneaker, with some money and the note reading, 'No Alohas'!

Chapter X
In Sometime

Memories and pain are like heavy luggage, you can't wait to drop them off somewhere or on someone, as a lot of people heading towards Sometime were waiting to do. Without the complications and heroin distractions and betrayal of Virginia and Judas, Becky was focused on getting to a town that she hated while growing up but wanted to see her mother and grandmother Wanda, then finding a place to drop off her heavy luggage from her experiences in Italy and her journey through Kansas and Missouri. She knew she was getting closer to Sometime when she opened her car windows and smelled cornfields along the roads, then remembered why she left the town because it smelled like corn, wet dogs, niggers and hatred!

Before going in Sometime, Becky got a room at the Crimes Pass Inn and without a guide or liaison, or their criminal pets, she carried her belongings into room #257 and locked her door because of what Virginia had said to her in the town of Solomon. She drank some scotch and took some more painkillers while she thought about the deaths of Gloria and Barabbas, and the unfortunate deaths of Virginia and Judas and how Sara was now an outlaw, then rested and had the best sleep she had in months. With the oncoming of the winter season a corn filled breeze blew through Becky's motel window, then waking up to a phone call from the man in the town of Solomon about Sara's whereabouts in the midwest, and that her grandmother Wanda Parker Black had died from grief and old age. The man from Solomon also told Becky that the Atticus Mercantile Store was sold by her father James Rollins, and after the death of her grandmother, Dahlia went up north to confront Ms. Sheila about a long time debt owed to her?

Before the winter set in on the 'anas' Rebeca was drinking 'herbal tea' at her Grandma Dean's home when the phone rang, and when the Spanish maid that looked after the house handed the phone to Rebeca, it was Becky on the other end telling her that she was in Sometime! They talked on the phone with long lost love and affection, then discussed how to get Sara and her daughter safely in Sometime?

Part I
The Outlaw Sara Blackfoot.

After the death of Tyrus Van Meter and the people from different parts of the 'anas' asking about her involvement in his death, Sara moved back up into the Canadian Territories with her aunt Josephine and married the first man that paid her any attention. She soon met and married a local man that was half Choctaw Indian named John Elkhorn and began having children, and while her husband did well working in certain casinos and her working as a surveyor, there were always problems with land and the people that thought they owned it. John Elkhorn was 6 foot, two inches tall and all of 235 pounds and had no problem displaying his prowess, being accused of beating up five white men in three separate casinos, and hanging an Elder from the Canadian Territories upside down on a rope from a large tree because he owed him 5 dollars. Sara had two boys and a girl with John Elkhorn with their names being John junior at 12 years old, Clinton, or 'Clint' as he was known being 10 years of age, and a girl named Rebeca who was seven. Sara was 35 years old when the 'territorial' wars became violent, and with liquor, casinos, gambling, drugs and prostitution abound like Sodom and Gomorrah, Sara wanted to take the family away from there but her husband refused, because his family owned land and he had a lot of money tied up in some real estate deals.

    The blood-lines of some races go back thousands of years but in a culture of greed and excess, money supersedes blood-lines and loyalty and that was the case for John Elkhorn, who owed some powerful people in the 'territories' money but refused to give up his family's land. On a blustery winter night some bad men came to John and Sara's home, demanding that he come outside to settle affairs and when he didn't come out of the house, the bad men started throwing Molotov Cocktails through the windows of the house while the kids were alone with her, causing Sara to shot at the men with her hunting rifle. Sara is an expert shot from her years of hunting and shot three of the bad men, with two of them dying from their wounds later that night in the hospital and the corrupt town sheriff issuing a warrant for her arrest for murder. John Elkhorn was in hiding but when he found out what happened to Sara and the kids, he went after some of the bad men and killed two of them before having a sit down meeting with some of the powerful 'Elders' of certain tribal families, while Sara gathered up the kids and went deep into the Canadian tundra to see her grandmother Agnes Blackfoot. Her grandmother was an 'Elder' of the Blackfoot Clan and was well-respected, with people coming as far as Russia to stop by her remote town to pay their respects to her before they went off to their lucrative fur trade. Sara told her grandmother what happened with the bad men and how she shot and killed two of them, and was **'Wanted'** for murder and had to leave her two sons with her because she was taking Rebeca to Sometime. A few days had passed as Sara explained to her three children what she was about to do, when Mrs. Agnes Blackfoot got news that John had been killed after the meeting with the 'Elders' of the 'territories' and told her granddaughter in private, while Sara's three children talked about their upcoming responsibilities and hugged each other.

The remote town of Moose Neck Bay gets cold very early and wakes its inhabitants up just as soon, when Sara saw her grandmother on the phone for a very long time and when she hung up, Sara asked her who she was talking to?

"I was talking with Mrs. Mildred Dean."

"Rebeca's grandmother, in Sometime?"

"Yes! Your **'Wanted'** from here to Kansas for murder, but me and Mrs. Dean talked about a plan to get you out of her to see Rebeca!"

"I have to leave the boys here with you for their own protection, but I'm taking Rebeca with me. Those bad men tried to kill me and my children and God knows what they did to my husband, but the ancient spirits will visit each one of them and they will be vanquished from the earth!"

"My child, you're leaving tomorrow on a small plane with Rebeca that will take you to a boat, and the boat will take you and Rebeca across Redemption Bay where you'll catch a cab to the airport, and once you and Rebeca get to the airport there will be two tickets for you. The tickets are in the name of 'Sara Dean' and once you reach the 'anas,' Mrs. Dean has arranged for you and Rebeca to be picked up and brought to the Dean Estate!"

"Do I have to swim across a river full of alligators with Rebeca on my back, or climb a mountain in the jungle with Rebeca on my back? As Becky would say, Christ in Jesus!"

"Don't get sassy with me young lady, you're the outlaw! I had my days in the sun and the boys will be fine, but you're right about those bad men. They will be wiped off the face of the earth, and their ancestors from the ground to the clouds in the sky will be ashamed of them!"

"I pray I don't have to kill someone before I get in Sometime!"

"Those things have already been taken care of! Now get some sleep, because you have to swim across a river and climb a mountain in the morning, all with Rebeca on your back??"

The cold early morning had Sara telling her boys she would see them a long time from now, and hugged her grandmother Agnes Blackfoot as she drank some 'herbal tea' and relit the 'peace pipe' that she was smoking from the night before. The **Outlaw** and **Wanted** posters began to blow away or were used for a stove fire, as Sara and Rebeca made all the trips that were told to her from her grandmother, until she was at the airport to get on a plane to the 'anas' with Rebeca?

Part II
The flow of the Wabash River.

The confidence she had was not the same when she had a guide or liaison, or their criminal pets, but when she left the Crimes Pass Inn she obliged an elderly couple with their granddaughter with a Polaroid in the lobby, then got into her car and followed the smell of the Wabash River along the roads to Sometime. As she drove along the Wabash River she remembered a teacher in school who told the class that the Wabash River was the 'little brother' of the Ohio River, and that many bad things happened along its banks. She remembered the overheard conversations between teachers at Sonoma High School about the racial killings, and how black and white bodies were thrown in the Wabash River, so that they could be washed out into the Ohio River and never be seen again.

She pulled over to stretch out her sore knee and have a cigarette with a sip of scotch before she followed the flow of the Wabash River, into Sometime, and as she stood by the rivers banks she thought about how the flow of the river could bring people good times, or wipe out everything they had because of the river's wrath. Some people from the 'anas' used to compare her basketball skills to that of the flowing of the Wabash River, because she was strong and consistent and giving to those around her, but had a wrath and destruction that only those close to her 'banks' could understand. Becky finished reminiscing about the

Wabash River and drove to the town of Nevertime and made a phone call to Grandma Dean's house. When she called and the Spanish maid answered the phone she handed it to Grandma Dean, who told Becky about her conversation with Sara's grandmother Agnes Blackfoot about getting her out of harm's way and made safe passage for them to the 'anas,' when Becky told her that she would be there soon and to tell Rebeca to 'Stay in the buggy' until she arrives! She left the town of Nevertime with suspicious looks from people and followed the flow of the Wabash River, knowing sooner or later she would start smelling reminders of the town she hated but as she drove closer to the town of Sometime, all she could smell was the flow of the Wabash River through her half opened car windows.

Part III
Safe passage and precious cargo.

Before Sara left on her epic journey to get in Sometime the word was already spread throughout the Canadian Territories and the 'anas' that Sara was carrying precious cargo, and was not to be harmed or serious retribution would be carried out on those that harmed the precious cargo, with Sara Blackfoot not being part of the deal? Her journey was almost as exaggerated as the ones she told her grandmother Agnes Blackfoot about swimming across a river full of alligators with Rebeca on her back, as a man tried to kidnap the precious cargo and kill the owner when they got to a remote place after getting off a boat. Another man killed the man that was trying to steal the precious cargo, making Sara not have to kill another man before she reached Sometime.

Once they reached the airport to take them to the 'anas' they were detained by certain people who were interested in the precious cargo, and if they knew anything about the outlaw Sara Blackfoot? Their arduous journey had come to a sad and unfortunate end from more bad men, and just as she was about to lose her precious cargo and never see Rebeca or Becky again, 10 white men and 7 Indians from the tribal territories in Canada, along with 5 Russian 'fur traders' that looked like they just escaped from the Gulag in Siberia went into the building that they were being held in. Within 2 hours of entering the building and some bodies that were going into The Wabash River, she got the plane to the 'anas' with her precious cargo and headed to the Dean family estate. It had been over a week since she left with the precious cargo and Grandma Dean was getting fidgety, walking around the house with her shotgun and tending to Rebeca, while her husband Jamison did what she told him to do and made sure that the tall black girl made it in Sometime also! It was well after midnight on a cold November evening when a loud knock came to the Dean family house, when Grandma Dean grabbed her shotgun to answer the door with flashbacks of the KKK doing the same things years ago, only without white hoods on their faces, and answered the door with the shotgun in her hand behind the door. The shady looking white man handed Grandma Dean a note then left with his Indian friend that was standing next to him, and once they got into the car to drive off Sara got out with the precious cargo, her seven year old daughter Rebeca.

Part IV
Little Women.

The arrival of the young girl brought a sense of relief and new found spirit to the Dean home, as everyone there had experienced personal tragedies in one way or another over the years, with the Spanish housekeeper crying with joy at the sight of the pretty girl and asking Sara if they needed anything? Grandma Dean hugged Sara and told them to get comfortable in the living-room, then went and picked up her shotgun by the door to make sure that the shady white man and Indian had driven off and when she closed the door, Rebeca came from her upstairs room to see what all the ruckus was about? When she came down the stairs and saw Sara she almost lost her balance and fell down the stairs, and when Sara ran to catch her from falling down the stairs and grabbed her by the arm, her and Rebeca sat in the middle of the stairway crying and wiping tears away from each other's eyes. They all assembled in the large living room adorned with some Elk and Moose heads mounted on the walls, when Sara introduced her daughter Rebeca LeeAnn Blackfoot to everyone in the living-room, which left a stunned and bewildered look on Grandma Dean and Rebeca's faces, and causing the Spanish housekeeper to say 'Jesus Christ' in Spanish before fainting and passing out on the living-room floor!

    The evening in the Dean home continued on into the early morning, with Grandma Dean talking to Mrs. Agnes Blackfoot on the phone about the safe passage of Sara and the 'precious cargo' of Rebeca to her home in Sometime, while Rebeca Dean stared at Sara and Rebeca while they slept on the couch. Most people in the 'anas' don't have alarm clocks in their bedrooms to wake them up, for they have an internal 'rooster clock' in their minds ever since they were children and before most rooster's crow at the break of sunlight, their up and beginning the days burdens or shot and killed the rooster that woke them up. The Spanish housekeeper recovered from her fainting episode and began checking on everyone, especially Rebeca Dean, and began making breakfast when there was another loud pounding on the door, causing Grandma Dean to pump her shotgun that she had already been cleaning since the break of dawn. At the door was Mr. Jamison Dean who came to tell his wife and daughter that Becky was in Sometime, but was holding a gun to the heads of a shady white man and an Indian who refused to let her onto the Dean Estate, telling a friend of Mr. Dean's that she came to see his daughter Rebeca and if she didn't, she would blow the two men's brains out and go back to Italy! After talking to his wife for a few minutes Mr. Dean left the house with a few men and before the rooster could crow again, a tall black figure walked through the Dean front door, causing the Spanish housekeeper to faint and pass out again!

When Rebeca Dean woke up from her nap and saw Becky sitting in a chair looking at her, she mustered up the remaining strength she had in her body to leap off from the couch and hug Becky so hard that she had a hard time breathing. The Spanish housekeeper recovered from yet another fainting spell and served them all breakfast in the living-room, with questions, tears, hugs, and more questions being mixed in with their food and the 'herbal tea' that was served to them, except for Rebeca Blackfoot who got orange juice.
"What's your name, little girl?"
"Rebeca LeeAnn Blackfoot, Ms. Becky."
"Christ in Jesus, she's got my middle name, you're a sneaky Indian girl, Sara!"
"Sneaky nothing, she's got my first name, so I get to tell her what to do about things! Rebeca, does anyone ever call you Becky?"
"No, Ms. Rebeca. Most people just call me Rebeca, why?"
"Just asking, because I hate it when people call me Becky, no offense, Becky!"
"None taken, besides, we should get the rules straight on what to call this little girl?"

"How about when you talk to her you call her 'little Becky,' and when I'm talking with her I'll call her 'little Rebeca,' sounds fair?"

"Sounds fair to me, Rebeca!"

"Don't I have a say in this, I'm her mother you know!"

"This doesn't concern you Sara, so let me and Becky continue talking about your daughter's name."

"What book are you reading, little Becky?"

"A book called Little Women by Louisa May Alcott, it's about four sisters who grew up with their mother in Massachusetts."

"I can get you some books by Zora Neale Hurston, have you ever heard of her?"

"Please don't start that Zora Neale Hurston shit with my daughter! That's how your mother, Ms. Dahlia Black, started all this traveling around the world and digging up stuff!"

It was now Grandma Dean at her home in Sometime living with her dying daughter Rebeca and her two lifelong friends Becky and Sara, along with Sara's daughter Rebeca and the occasionally fainting Spanish housekeeper to watch out for each other against death and bad people. The other Dean children would stop by the house on occasion and were taken by the gathering of such a motley crew in their parents' home, with some people throughout the 'anas' beginning to gossip about the 'tall, rich nigger and Indian outlaw and murderer' living in the Dean family home, not to mention that Rebeca had killed her father some years back and a small 'outlaw' child was also living there! Grandma Dean accepted an invitation from Mrs. Agnes Blackfoot to come up into the remote part of the Canadian tundra as her guest, with the stipulation that Ms. Ling Kwan was present as a guest also, which Grandma Dean accepted and made preparations to go back to where Sara and Rebeca had come from.

Part V
Like the book.

She went by car, boat, and plane to meet Mrs. Agnes Blackfoot and Ms. Ling Kwan in the remote area by Moose Head Bay and when they met, the three 'Elders' of their Clans settled all disputes from the past over 'herbal tea' and a peace pipe that Mrs. Blackfoot relit from the night before. While her grandmother was up in Sara's neck of the woods,

Rebeca Dean made arrangements to have Becky, Sara and 'little Rebeca' stay on the property with small houses of their own so they could be close to her while she dealt with her debilitating cancer ordeal. Within a few days they all settled into their new 'homes' on the Dean Family Estate but always went over to the main house to spend time with Rebeca, realizing 'why' they had endured all they had been through when they saw their 'spunky' friend that sacrificed her life to take their advice and kill her father, slowly dying of ovarian cancer and suffering her pain every day at her bedside, while Rebeca sat with them and continued to read her book Little Women.

The weather was getting colder and the late year holidays of Thanksgiving and Christmas were upon most parts of the world, when news came to the Dean family home that Mr. Jamison Dean had died of a heart attack while trying to kill a man half his age, which caused the Spanish housekeeper to cry with joy and not faint or pass out because she hated the man. Grandma Dean came back to Sometime with the assurances from Mrs. Agnes Blackfoot and Ms. Ling Kwan that her motley crew of 'little women' would live in peace, in exchange for some land and a pact to have the bad men that killed John Elkhorn and tried to kill his wife and children wiped off the face of the earth. The funeral for Mr. Jamison Dean was a testament to a devout Pentecostal man, as many people from the 'anas' came to pay their respects or spit on his casket as he was laid to rest in an unknown grave, for fear that people who hated him would dig up his bones and kick them around the cemetery or the streets and tarnish his legacy.

    They gathered in the Dean family home every day and night and dealt with the hardships of life in the world and with each other, bonding with each other for all the years they missed together and Grandma Dean watching over them, causing young Rebeca to refer to her 'other' grandmother as 'Marmee' from the book she was reading. Living in the home at the time seemed like they were all under house arrest, with no one venturing too far from the compound on the Dean Estate except for necessary things that were taken care of by people loyal to Grandma Dean, which she left in the charge of the oft fainting and passing out Spanish housekeeper. For the well-worn Becky and Sara it was a beautiful reprieve from the journey's they had experienced, going through all they suffered just to get back into the town they both hated and swore they would never return to again, only to suffer the hardships to see their friend Rebeca Stanwyck Dean. Since the arrival of her two dearest friends Rebeca's health and spirits picked up, becoming as feisty as she used to be when she was on the Aianta Cliff or in Dire, and ordered a large Christmas tree be brought into the house and made a list of presents to be brought to young Rebeca for Christmas. The holiday season for the end of that year was melancholy at best, with everyone in the house having lost someone to death, or being the cause of it, young Rebeca wrote in her diary in the living-room as Grandma Dean, Rebeca, Sara, Becky and the Spanish housekeeper sipped 'herbal tea' and shared stories, when Grandma Dean asked young Rebeca what she was writing in her book? She told Grandma Dean that she was writing about everyone in the house, and how the way they were living was like the book she was reading.

Chapter XI
Peace With Aianta

In the final days of everyone's life they have to make peace with something or someone, and Rebeca Stanwyck Dean was making peace with those around her, but most importantly with herself. They all decided to be with Rebeca 'til death do us part' and spent most of their time behaving like the young girls they used to be on the Aianta Cliff, having little camp outs in the woods and putting make-up on Rebeca as Sara talked about her Cheyenne heritage and wandered her eyes for something to kill, occasionally making 'bunny chicken' which always made Becky throw up. One day after the start of the new year in 1986 Grandma Dean spoke with Mrs. Agnes Blackfoot with news about Sara's two boys John, jr. and Clinton, telling Grandma Dean that they were fine and both were sent off to remote places, with John, jr. going with some Russian fur traders to become a merchant and Clint being raised by an uncle that was an Elder of the Blackfoot Clan. A cold March night brought the women inside the Dean home, with Becky and Rebeca talking about what school young Rebeca should go to, and telling Sara that the conversations about 'their' daughter didn't concern her, when they came into the house and saw Grandma Dean watching a Celtics game with Larry Bird's grandmother and sipping 'herbal tea' while cursing at the television set.

Grandma Dean gave Sara the news about her two sons and with relief, she looked at her daughter and told her that she would see her two brothers a time from now, then looked at Becky and Rebeca and told them, "This is my home now, my sons are men and will visit me in the next life! I pray they don't shame their ancestors in this lifetime or the next!" They all soon began to gather in the living-room to watch the Boston Celtics and Larry Bird on television, with everyone in the room having their different opinions about the games and Becky commentating about what Bird should or should not do in basketball games, and the women trying to prevent Grandma Dean and Larry Bird's grandmother from shooting the television set with their shotguns over bad calls! The Dean Estate gave the young Rebeca an Eden in her life as she rode her horse 'Little Gunsmoke' around the compound and tended to her own little patch of chickens, goats, rabbits, horses, roosters and cows, and learning how to shot different types of guns from the women in the house just in case the Klu Klux Klan showed up on their doorstep unannounced! It was surprising to everyone that despite Rebeca's cancer treatments she never lost any of her long brown hair, sometimes holding up a picture of her mother Dorothy and standing next to Grandma Dean to see who looked more like Barbara Stanwyck, with Dorothy's picture winning all the time and young Rebeca asking the women in the house 'who Larry Bird was'?

They were gathered in the living-room after spending the day together on the Aianta Cliff, when young Rebeca mentioned getting a Buddha statue for the house because it would bring wellness and good spirits into the home and after hearing what young Rebeca had said, they all agreed to go look for a Buddhist statue the next day. In the other part of the house that was separated by a patch of land the size of a football field, Grandma Dean and her new guest Mrs. Agnes Blackfoot, along with the Spanish housekeeper, talked in the 'Den of Elders' about the death of Ling Kwan and the deaths of the rest of the bad men that tried to kill Sara's two sons, while sharing 'herbal tea' and smoking the peace pipe that Mrs. Agnes Blackfoot brought with her from the tundra of Moose Neck Bay.

The next morning saw a bright sun rise over the Dean Estate and Rebeca in good spirits and health as they all got together and prepared themselves to find a Buddhist statue, as Grandma Dean, Mrs. Agnes Blackfoot and the Spanish housekeeper were having breakfast and coffee in the other part of the house yards away while cleaning and polishing their guns, just in case there were unexpected knocks on the door while the Spanish housekeeper watched them leave the property through binoculars in between sips of her coffee. They all drove in a large black pick-up truck that could fit a family and with young Rebeca driving the truck on a stack of old bibles and Yellow Pages phone books, Becky and Sara sat in the backseat arguing about where to find a Buddhist statue, as Rebeca sat in the front seat with young Rebeca and pointed out all the places that she hated while growing up in Sometime then pulled out a hairbrush to do young Rebeca's hair while they were stopped at a redlight, when Becky reached her long black arm to the front seat and slapped the hairbrush out of Rebeca's hand, telling her that it wasn't 'Barbara Stanwyck' all over again!

Part I
Buddha on Lotus.

Many roads lead to one thing, a destination, and as young Rebeca drove the truck through a couple of roads bouncing up and down on a stack of old bibles and telephone books, they came across a flower shop with a large Buddha statue in the front window and immediately pulled over to the store, with Becky and Sara checking their guns in their pocketbooks before leaving the car. They went into the Vintao Flower Shop and the small Himalayan woman that owned the store greeted them, grabbing Rebeca's hand and looking up at Becky while praying for them all and telling them that she knew of their ancestors. The caramel complexion of the old Himalayan woman with long gray hair surprised them all, as she looked like she never aged except for wisdom and pointed her hands towards the books and flowers that were in her store, with young Rebeca fixated on the Buddha statue in the window. They walked through the small bookstore with Becky having to bend down a little because of her height and picked out books to their liking, with Rebeca getting a book on meditation, Becky grabbing a book from the top shelf on Italian cooking, and Sara reading a book about General George Custer and the massacre at Little BigHorn. While they went through their books, young Rebeca asked the old woman what the statue represented and if she could have it?

The woman in a wise way told the inquisitive young Rebeca that precious gifts have no value, and that the Buddha on Lotus statue represented the Buddha praying for happiness and wellbeing while floating on a lotus flower down a river. She told the old Himalayan woman how she needed the statute for the happiness and wellbeing of everyone that lived in the house she was living in, and when the old woman knew she was protected with the blessings of Ling Kwan, Agnes Blackfoot and Grandma Dean, she order three men to remove the three foot and weighing nearly 200 pound statute from the front of the window and have it loaded on the back of their truck.

When they got their books and realized what young Rebeca had done to get the Buddha on Lotus statue, Rebeca and Becky offered the old Himalayan woman a large sum of money which she refused and looked at them as if she had been insulted, while Sara understood the meaning of precious gifts and hugged the woman in a Cheyenne Indian custom then left the store with her 'little women' posse as the three men loaded the Buddha statue on the back of the truck. Sara Blackfoot drove the truck on the way back to the Dean Estate as her daughter sat next to her in the front seat, with Becky and Rebeca discussing 'what' young Rebeca said to the old Himalayan woman to give her a Buddha on Lotus statue?

Part II
West of Eden.

The Buddha statue was the centerpiece of the Dean home and was placed in the middle of a large Bay window in the living-room, having a God-like presence when the sun rose and faded behind it while they spent time together during the day keeping Rebeca company and playing many board games. They were all sitting in the living-room watching the movie *East of Eden* with James Dean and Rebeca constantly mentioning that she was related to him, when Grandma Dean came into the living-room with the Spanish housekeeper and told them that Agnes Blackfoot had died of a heart attack while praying.

They stopped watching the movie and eating their snacks when Sara thanked Grandma Dean for telling her about her grandmother's death, then began to excuse herself from the living-room and telling young Rebeca that they had to leave, so they could go up north and pay their respects to Agnes Blackfoot. Grandma Dean stepped in front of her, with the Spanish housekeeper doing the same, and told her that neither her or young Rebeca were going anywhere because her grandmother didn't die up north, but in her house a few yards away while they shared memories and herbal tea. Everyone in the living-room were shocked, especially Sara and young Rebeca, because none of them knew that Mrs. Agnes Blackfoot was actually staying in the town of Sometime only a couple yards away?

With the passing of her grandmother and her 'rank' elevated in the family, Sara was now an 'Elder' of the Blackfoot Clan and wanted her grandmother's body sent to the frozen tundra of Moose Neck Bay to be buried, but Grandma Dean told her that Agnes Blackfoot was already buried in an unmarked grave so that people wouldn't dig up her bones and disgrace her memory. With the passing of Agnes Blackfoot, it was apparent that the young Rebeca LeeAnn Blackfoot had to be groomed properly for the society that awaited her, as Becky and Rebeca continued to debate about which school young Rebeca should go too, either Aurora or Sonoma schools and when the new 'Elder' of the Blackfoot Clan tried to express her opinion about where her daughter should go to school, she was politely told that the conversation didn't concern her?? Because of her worldwide status and being the best basketball player that the 'anas' ever produced, some would argue regarding the Bird fella, Becky won the debate and it was decided that young Rebeca was going to enroll at Sonoma Middle School during the Fall semester and while young Rebeca's future was being planned for her, Rebeca was taking a toll for the not so better.

Her illness was not a burden for anyone in the house because they understood 'why' they went through what they did to see her, and what she did to save their lives and could feel her pain every day as she suffered from the 'invisible monster from within' like Christ, all the while maintaining a feisty spirit and a head full of long brown hair, which young Rebeca brushed for her every day. She was a beautiful almost ten year old girl with long black and brown hair down to her shoulders and brownish-green eyes, with a slight cut over her left eye during a hunting trip and was already good at shooting and using a knife. Grandma Dean told her that she 'sprouts like a weed' because she was already five-feet, two inches tall and had beautiful calloused hands like her mother, and only got a shade less brown during the winter months. They called hear by many names in the house and she knew the distinct voices of everyone that called for her, with Becky and Rebeca cling her 'little Becky' or 'little Rebeca,' her mother calling her 'Becka,' Grandma Dean calling her 'My child,' and the Spanish housekeeper referring to her as 'Chica'?

The ten year old Rebeca LeeAnn Blackfoot was learning the wisdom and strength from some very powerful women, who would gather around the Budda statue at night sharing 'herbal tea' and the peace pipe that Mrs. Agnes Blackfoot brought with her from Moose Head Bay and have discussions about how they shot and killed people and who had it coming, or when negros were cut down from trees and the ruthlessness of Ling Kwan! None of the stories that the young girl heard affected her in a negative way, as most of the women in the living-room had killed someone in their lifetime, or had someone killed in their lifetime, and the Spanish housekeeper telling them in Spanish how she killed seven men while escaping the revolution that happened in her country, and lost two children and a sister during her struggle to get to Sometime with the help of Grandma Dean and Ling Kwan!

Her room was filled with white and blue lotus flowers and as the 'invisible monster from within' caused her to suffer more pain to her already painful life, Rebeca sat in her room on a rainy day and reading Genesis in the bible about the Garden of Eden as young Rebeca brushed her now shorter brown hair and asked her where she wanted to be buried?

"I want to be buried on Aianta Cliff where I first met Becky and your mother. We thought we could spend the rest of our lives on that cliff, and Sara actually did for a while!"

"Aunty Rebeca, where is Aianta Cliff?"

"It's west of a town called Eden and hangs out over the town, dictating the shade of the sun and moon over the town. There are some places on the cliff that have the pretty trees my mother loved, and caves we could hide in, if Becky could get her long legs into them, to get away from troubled people!"

"Aunty Rebeca, why did you kill your father?"

"Like your mother and Becky told me on the cliff, 'or he'll kill you,' that's why I killed Tyrus Van Meter! He never loved my mother as much as he loved me, and she got put in a mental hospital?'"

"Aunty Rebeca, promise me something?"

"What's that, little Rebeca?"

"Promise me that you, my mother, Aunt Becky, Grandma Dean, and the Spanish housekeeper don't turn me into a mental patient, or a girl who has a tendency to shoot someone when they're wronged or slighted?"

"I don't think you'll have that problem little Rebeca, we've suffered enough deaths to last a lifetime, but it doesn't hurt to carry a buck knife with you, just ask your mother!"

"I'm going to miss you, Aunty Rebeca.."

"I'm going to miss me too, but when my life is taken as the good Lord sees fit, I'm glad I lived long enough to see 'our' daughter and how people came from all across the world, and some people dying in the process just to see me, the girl who killed her father!"

"Does everyone in the house know you want to be buried West of Eden?"

"Yes they do, and be careful with that hairbrush! Are you trying to brush out the rest of my hair? Do you think I look like Barbara Stanwyck, the movie actress?"

Part III
Last Moon over Aianta Cliff.

The Moon has an effect on everything that exists on earth and many cultures celebrate its power in different ways, with its icy cool stare from the sky it brings harvest and rebirth, calmness to the waters around the world and the power to make people lunatics! It rained one night as the women of the Dean house sat outside and chatted amongst each other when Grandma Dean grabbed everyone's hand and baptized them in the rain, when Sara noticed the 'Death Moon' in the sky and knew that Rebeca didn't have long to live. The information for the women came through the Dean house and Becky got a telegram from her mother Dahlia, explaining to her that she was teaching Anthropology at Chicago University and that her father James Rollins settled with a woman named Lynnette in Calumet, Illinois and the whereabouts of Ms. Sheila was unknown.

They had survived the hardships of death, bonding, sickness and isolation, and the month of April carried with it the rebirth of many things, but also the 'Death Moon' at night that balances everything out. They were all getting together at the Dean house to go to church on the third Friday of April, when the Spanish housekeeper told 'Chica' to go check on Rebeca and see if she was going to church? When young Rebeca went into Rebeca's room filled with white and blue lotus flowers, she was sitting in a chair by the window with a hairbrush in her hand and had finally succumbed to the cancer and pain in her life…

They buried her three days later West of Eden, on a remote part of Aianta Cliff near a cave she loved that was surrounded by pretty trees during the last moon of Aianta, and all of them making their peace with God and Rebeca on the cliff of Aianta before they left the small headstone for her.

Rebeca S. Dean
Born October 13, 1952-Died April 3, 1987
Our Friend

After Rebeca's passing the women stayed close to each other but were living in separate parts of the midwest, with Becky and Sara starting a real estate business called Sometime Realtors and Grandma Dean and the Spanish housekeeper sharing 'herbal teas' and occasionally the peace pipe from Agnes Blackfoot. Rebeca LeeAnn Blackfoot enrolled at Sonoma Middle School and quickly became friends with a scrappy white girl from Wichita, Kansas that lived with her aunt in Sometime named Edith Winter. They shared classes and conversations together while in school, with Edith Winter telling young Rebeca how she hated her father while they took the trash out together in between a thin wired fence at the school.

The End.

About the Author

The author of *Love songs, Haikus, and other lies, The Color of Onyx, The Slave Master's Son, and Writings from Judah.* The author has just completed his first book, *Becky. A tale of two girls,* and is currently working on a second book, *The Outside of Onyx.*
   Currently lives in Boston , Massachusetts.

www.ingramcontent.com/pod-product-compliance
Lightning Source LLC
LaVergne TN
LVHW041706060526
838201LV00043B/608